W9-BSP-369

# When Had A Woman Turned Him Down?

Jake's pulse quickened. He hadn't found love in thirty-two years, and he didn't think he would in time to get what he wanted. He needed a wife to start a family with as quickly as possible. "I've been thinking about my future, Emily. And I've come to a decision. We should think about a marriage of convenience."

"Marriage!" she gasped.

"That's right. A marriage entered into with calm heads and logical planning. A marriage that will satisfy our needs, yet remain practical. We've worked together for several years. It's ideal."

"It's preposterous!" she exclaimed.

"It's perfect," he said, taking her hand in his. "Emily, will you marry me?"

Dear Reader,

Marriage—a legal union that can be the best and most joyous relationship, or it can be as volatile as dynamite in a burning building. When two contrasting forces are locked together in a marriage of convenience the relationship loses all convenience, and sparks fly.

I was interested in a story with characters whose goals in life were totally different. As you turn the pages of *Wed to the Texan,* you will meet Jake Thorne, a commanding, handsome billionaire who is impelled to obtain even more riches, and Emily Carlisle, whose purpose in life is to help others.

Jake is a driven, strong-willed charmer who will use deceit to add to his fortune…until he meets Emily, who is unlike any other woman he's known. While their passion rages hot and wild, the clash of wills is fierce. In spite of their differences, the two cannot resist each other.

Thank you for your interest in the PLATINUM GROOMS: Jake, and his friends Nick and Ryan.

*Sara Orwig*

# SARA ORWIG

# WED TO THE TEXAN

Published by Silhouette Books
**America's Publisher of Contemporary Romance**

If you purchased this book without a cover you should be aware
that this book is stolen property. It was reported as "unsold and
destroyed" to the publisher, and neither the author nor the
publisher has received any payment for this "stripped book."

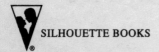

**SILHOUETTE BOOKS**

ISBN-13: 978-0-373-76887-5
ISBN-10:     0-373-76887-7

WED TO THE TEXAN

Copyright © 2008 by Sara Orwig

All rights reserved. Except for use in any review, the reproduction
or utilization of this work in whole or in part in any form by any
electronic, mechanical or other means, now known or hereafter
invented, including xerography, photocopying and recording, or in
any information storage or retrieval system, is forbidden without
the written permission of the editorial office, Silhouette Books,
233 Broadway, New York, NY 10279 U.S.A.

This is a work of fiction. Names, characters, places and incidents are
either the product of the author's imagination or are used fictitiously, and
any resemblance to actual persons, living or dead, business establishments,
events or locales is entirely coincidental.

This edition published by arrangement with Harlequin Books S.A.

® and TM are trademarks of Harlequin Books S.A., used under license.
Trademarks indicated with ® are registered in the United States Patent
and Trademark Office, the Canadian Trade Marks Office and in other
countries.

Visit Silhouette Books at www.eHarlequin.com

**Printed in U.S.A.**

R0414538564

**Recent books by Sara Orwig**

Silhouette Desire

*Shut Up and Kiss Me #1581
*Standing Outside the Fire #1594
Estate Affair #1657
†Pregnant with the First Heir #1752
†Revenge of the Second Son #1757
†Scandals from the Third Bride #1762
Seduced by the Wealthy Playboy #1813
‡Pregnant at the Wedding #1864
‡Seduced by the Enemy #1875
‡Wed to the Texan #1887

Silhouette Intimate Moments

*Bring on the Night #1298
*Don't Close Your Eyes #1316

*Stallion Pass: Texas Knights
†The Wealthy Ransomes
‡Platinum Grooms

## SARA ORWIG

lives in Oklahoma. She has a patient husband, who will take her on research trips anywhere from big cities to old forts. She is an avid collector of Western history books. With a master's degree in English, Sara has written historical romance, mainstream fiction and contemporary romance. Books are beloved treasures that take Sara to magical worlds, and she loves both reading and writing them.

To Melissa and Maureen and other angels in my life—
thank you, thank you for being there!

# Prologue

To get what he wanted, Jake Thorne knew he had to marry soon. Shifting uneasily in his brown leather desk chair, he gazed out the twenty-fifth-story office window. Tall buildings, then trees and homes filled the distance until the horizon blended with the Dallas sky. How was he going to find a wife who suited him in the next few weeks?

There were plenty of women in his life, but none he had a shred of interest in developing a long-term relationship with—much less marrying. Particularly under the circumstances. Too many of them only wanted a luxurious life and social status. His last relationship had ended miserably and resulted in dating burnout. If he married, he had to find someone who wasn't after his money and all that went with it.

Jake's thoughts were interrupted by one of his secretaries on the intercom asking if he could sign some papers. As Emily

Carlisle entered, he gave her a swift glance and realized her brown hair had grown long enough to pile on her head. He'd long ago thought she might as well come to work in a uniform. As far as he knew, her entire wardrobe consisted of cotton blouses and straight skirts in bland colors. Functional and attractive like wallpaper, she blended into the office decor. He paid little attention to her except over matters concerning his work. He did know the glasses she wore were fake. Once, when he'd quizzed her about going without them half of the time, she admitted she bought them to make herself look older. Emily was quiet, pleasant and one of the most efficient secretaries he had, so he didn't care if she came to work wearing burlap. Although she'd worked for him for several years, he had no idea if there was a man in her life. Nor did he care.

She brought a stack of letters and reports to him, which he gave a cursory glance and began to sign. As soon as he was finished, she handed him a couple of pink slips.

"You have two calls. The messages were on my machine when I arrived this morning. Kalas Jaskowski and Miranda Gable."

"Set a phone appointment with Jaskowski," he said.

Miranda was probably inviting him to one of her parties and would like to rekindle a relationship he had no interest in. "Tell Miranda I'm leaving soon for Australia and I'll call her when I return. I'll be out of the country for two weeks starting next week on the first of February."

"The trip is on your calendar," Emily replied, and then reminded him of his schedule for the day, listing his meetings.

"Later today, when I've finished my appointments, I want to shut myself in here. I have contracts to go over and a report to write. I don't want any calls or interruptions and I'll need some typing done."

"Fine," she said, gathering papers. He forgot about her before she was even out of the room.

It was late in the afternoon when Jake's last appointment finished and he had his office to himself again. Finally he'd have solitude to read the contracts. He still had typing for Emily to do, and he realized he was keeping her overtime, but she'd said it didn't matter.

At six, Jake grabbed his gray suit coat and headed for the door. He was surprised to spot Emily still busy at her computer. He strode over to her desk. "We're through, Emily. Go home."

She smiled. "I'm getting something ready for morning."

He reached down and pulled the plug on her computer. "Get your things. I'll take you to dinner with me."

Emily's wide blue eyes looked startled. "You don't need to—"

"I know I don't. Are you free this evening?"

"Yes," she replied, "but really, dinner isn't necessary."

"I want to." To his amusement, she appeared to be debating with herself. He couldn't recall a woman doing that since he was thirteen years old and wanted a neighbor girl to go to a school dance. "It's just dinner, Emily," he added.

She blushed, getting her purse out of her desk and coming to join him, while gazing at him with a perplexed look as if he had sprouted another head.

"There isn't a man in your life who'll mind if we have dinner together, is there?" he asked.

"Not at all," she snapped. He wondered if she was as soured on dating as he was.

While he held the door, she strolled through ahead of him

and he caught a faint whiff of a pleasant perfume. His gaze slid down her back. Covered by her black jacket and long dark-green skirt, he could tell little about her body. But with the urgent need to find a wife on his mind, he stared more intently at Emily.

Proposing to her was a preposterous idea. They were worlds apart in lifestyles. But as he walked her to his car, he reconsidered. In his elegant, black, four-door Maserati he shed his suit coat and tie and unfastened the top buttons of his shirt. Most women gushed over his expensive luxury cars. Emily's cool expression indicated mild disapproval. How intriguing! What kind of woman could ignore his money?

At the steakhouse they sat and Jake ordered a bottle of wine. When they were alone, he reached across the table to take off her fake glasses and hand them to her. "I know you don't need these," he said. Her blue eyes, with their thick lashes were beautiful. She had shed her jacket, and while her beige cotton blouse was loose-fitting, it was shapely enough for him to realize she had some curves.

Smiling at him, she put away the glasses. "I forget I'm wearing them. You're right, I don't need them."

"So tell me about yourself. How do you spend your free time? I gather there's no man in your life right now."

"No, and there won't be one for a while. Things didn't work out well the last time," she said with a note of bitterness. "Maybe I expect too much."

"Like what?"

She shrugged. "Someone compatible. A person I enjoy being with. A man who likes my family."

"Ah, so family is important to you. You hope to marry and have your own family someday. Right?"

"It's the most important thing in life," she said, and then bit her lip. "I suppose it's not to you. I know professional success means a lot to you. You work almost around the clock and through the weekends."

"Money and career are important, but I want marriage and children, too," he said, speculating. "I don't always keep my nose to the grindstone," he added with amusement, thinking about his yacht and mountain home. "Tell me about your family."

Her father was a minister, both her parents lived in Dallas, and she had three married brothers and one married sister. She drank only a sip of her wine and continued to talk through tossed salads. She was making no particular effort to charm him and definitely none to come on to him. There was no flirting, no fire, just friendly conversation—the same as at the office. She didn't seem interested in his fortune. He found out she was thirty, only a bit younger than he was, but that didn't matter. She had already proved herself reliable, trustworthy and intelligent. Not the qualities he usually sought in the women he took out, but perhaps that was part of his problem in finding one he could tolerate long enough to propose to.

To Jake's amusement, Emily asked for a box to take home her leftovers, something he hadn't done since he'd received his first six-figured check. He'd stopped being thrifty and never intended to be again.

As they left the restaurant, he took her arm. "The night's still young. Let me show you my house. We can have a brandy and continue our conversation."

"Thank you, but I have to go home," she said, glancing up at him. "I have a long day tomorrow. I'm a math tutor at my church."

When had a woman turned down an offer to see his house? His pulse quickened. Had he found the solution to his dilemma? Love would have no part in the equation. He hadn't found love in thirty-two years and he didn't think he would in time to get what he wanted. He needed a wife to start a family with as quickly as possible.

"I live on Oak Avenue in an apartment complex," she said.

"You live close to the office."

"Within walking or cycling distance," she answered, smiling at him.

He knew he would never get invited inside her apartment, so when he turned into the wide driveway, he parked, switched off the ignition and shifted to face her. "Emily, you sound as burned out on relationships as I am."

"I suppose so," she replied.

"Yet we both want marriage and a family. Right?"

"Yes," she answered with a faint smile, unbuckling her seat belt and facing him. Her hand reached for the door handle.

"I've been thinking about my future, Emily. And getting to know you better tonight, I've come to a decision. We should think about a marriage of convenience. I think we could make a marriage work. It would give us both what we want."

"Marriage!" she gasped, staring at him with huge eyes. Her mouth hung open, and he noticed her lips were curved, full and inviting.

"That's right. A marriage entered into with calm heads and logical planning. A marriage that will satisfy our needs, yet remain practical and easy. Convenient. We've worked together for several years now, so we're definitely not strangers. It's ideal."

"It's preposterous!" she exclaimed.

"No, it's perfect," Jake announced, taking her hand in his. It was soft, her skin smooth as satin. Feeling more certain by the minute about his decision, he gazed into her blue eyes. "Emily, will you marry me?"

# One

*Seventeen months later*

Palm fronds swayed in the gentle breeze as sunlight splashed over Jake's sprawling white stucco villa. Standing on the veranda, Emily gazed at the sparkling jewel of a blue swimming pool with its waterfalls and fountains. Lavish landscaping with a velvet green lawn and exotic tropical flowers in immaculate beds surrounded the pool. The beach and blue ocean lay farther out. Back home in Dallas, September meant summer was still hanging on, but here the ocean breezes cooled the late afternoon. Her husband's private island should have been a paradise, not a prison. Yet Emily wanted to get back to Texas. Jake would be home any minute and she would have to confront him with her plans.

The beauty of her surroundings was lost on her while she

mulled over her options. For seventeen months she had been locked in a marriage of convenience. But now she was ready to break her vows. She couldn't be the woman Jake needed. Yet reluctance tore at her.

She'd had enough of island life. Jake was flying off the island to work every day, so he probably hadn't missed Dallas or even noticed the difference. But this leisurely life of doing nothing wasn't for her. Any more than it would have been for Jake.

The roar of one of Jake's sport cars announced his arrival. Emily turned, stepping inside the house to wait. Ceiling fans revolved lazily above the casual bamboo furniture. A floor-to-ceiling mirror showed her reflection and she turned to check out how she looked.

Her long brown hair was tied with a silk ribbon behind her head and she wore a bright blue cotton sundress and sandals. She'd lost weight. Jake hadn't noticed, but that didn't surprise her.

As she waited, she heard the front door and the click of Jake's shoes on the polished hardwood floor. She called to him and he strode into the room, tossing his cell phone and keys onto a table. Her pulse jumped at the sight of him.

This intense reaction to him had developed during the whirlwind courtship before their wedding. When she'd worked for him, she'd known that her boss was a handsome, sexy man. But once he focused his attention on her, her response to him had intensified, something she was less than happy about. She didn't want Jake capturing her heart as he had so many other females'.

She remembered the calls he used to get at the office, the women who'd stop by unannounced, trying to get him to take them back into his life. She'd hoped she would never act that way with any man. That she'd never act that way with Jake.

He was tall with perfectly trimmed black hair. But it was his thickly lashed, smoke-colored eyes that set her heartbeat racing. His firm jaw, straight nose and high cheekbones added to the rugged, appealing face that turned heads everywhere he went. It would be impossible for him to enter any room and not be noticed. Dressed in one of his brown tailor-made suits, which she had been appalled to discover cost two thousand dollars, he exuded success and self-assurance. She tried to keep banked a smoldering flame of desire because she'd reached a turning point in their unstable marriage. She dreaded the next hour, but she had to face the future.

"You look wonderful. It's so nice to be home," he announced, striding up to embrace her. His aftershave was faint, but masculine and tempting. It reminded her of the muscled body beneath the elegant suit. "Hey! Why the long face?" he asked, tilting up her chin.

"Jake, I want to talk," she said. She heard the breathless note in her voice and wondered if she could go through with her rehearsed speech. His arms were strong, holding her pressed against him and as usual, her determination began to waver. He was gorgeous. He had all sorts of wonderful qualities, yet she was miserable every day. She felt as if she was failing him because she couldn't give him the baby he wanted.

"So do I. Although I thought we could talk later and make love now," he said in a husky voice. He caressed her neck and throat, stirring sizzles of pleasure through her, increasing her racing heartbeat. He fished in his pocket. "I brought you a present."

She inhaled and stared at a long slender black box tied with a red satin ribbon. "You shouldn't get these gifts for me," she said.

"I don't know why not. I want to. Open it," he commanded with a note of eagerness in his voice. She gazed up into his eyes and saw dancing flames of desire in their depths.

Wriggling out of his embrace, she tugged the ribbon free, opened the package and lifted out a black velvet box. When she raised the lid, a dazzling diamond-and-sapphire necklace sparkled in the afternoon light. "It's gorgeous," she said flatly, disappointment washing over her.

He tilted up her chin. "What's wrong? You sound as if I've given you a bunch of weeds."

"It's beautiful, Jake. It's not the necklace. We have to talk. There's something wrong here. Not the necklace. It's other things—this marriage we have." She inhaled deeply, gazing into his unfathomable eyes. She knew most women would never do what she was about to do. Her sister, Beth, had spent hours on the phone arguing with her about it. "Our marriage, our…deal—it's not working."

Jake frowned. "Give it a chance. We've only been married for a little over a year and a half. What exactly aren't you happy about?"

"We agreed we wanted a baby. We've been to doctors who've said we're both healthy, but I'm not getting pregnant. I feel as if I'm failing you."

"Relax. Give it time," Jake said, his voice lowering and his frown vanishing. "In fact, we can work on it tonight," he said, nuzzling her neck.

She almost closed her eyes and succumbed as she had so many times before. Jake was passionate, understanding and constantly trying to please her—he was impossible to resist. But for once, she clung to her sanity, grasped his arms and leaned away from him.

"Jake, listen to me!" she demanded. "You know you can distract me, but we need to talk about this."

Jake stroked her cheek lightly. "Darlin', I've tried to give you everything you want. You can spend your time as you please. I'll tell you what—go change and we'll fly to Grand Cayman for dinner and dancing. You've been on this island a month, and it's time to get you out. While you dress, I'll have the plane readied and we can talk all evening." He walked to the hall table and picked up his cell phone. "I'll make dinner reservations," he called over his shoulder.

"Jake, we can stay right here…"

"I know we *can,* but I want to take you out. How long will it take you to get ready?"

"Ten minutes," she said, shaking her head, wondering how a man who was so brilliant in business could be so dense about relationships.

"Make it fifteen so I can shower and shave." He turned, flipped open his phone and started talking as she stared at the empty doorway.

"This is part of what I'm talking about," she said to no one. "You aren't listening. You're just doing exactly what you want to do." Clamping her lips together, she headed to their spacious bedroom to change. She could already hear Jake in the shower.

In the walk-in closet that was larger than half of her old apartment, Emily set the necklace and its open velvet box on the hand-crafted walnut triple dresser, stared at the brilliant diamonds and deep blue sapphires and sighed. So many women would be thrilled to get a gift like this.

As she dressed she could hear the waves hitting the beach through the open glass doors. A paradise and a prison. That was all her island home was. Her marriage, too.

She guessed they would eat in a luxurious dining room, so she selected a deep blue, sleeveless sheath. Prim and plain, it had tiny ebony buttons that fastened to the high, round collar. The lines were simple, yet the dress suited her. She brushed her hair again, looping and pinning it on top of her head. She wore little makeup, so after slipping on high-heeled sandals and grabbing her envelope silk purse, she was ready to join Jake. She paused to stare at the diamond-and-sapphire necklace. As far as she was concerned, it was too elegant for tonight. She picked up a diamond drop he'd given her and put it on, watching it sparkle against the blue dress. She didn't care about jewelry and seldom wore it, but she knew it pleased Jake when she wore his gifts.

As she hurried through the villa, she wondered whether she would ever be able to get him to listen to her. Maybe she should just walk out and leave him a letter.

Jake stood by the front door looking at his BlackBerry. At the sight of him, her pulse jumped. Whatever else, her husband was handsome. Dressed in a tailor-made navy suit and a monogrammed white shirt, he looked like the successful billionaire he was.

Jake's chiseled features and prominent cheekbones always made her heart skip a beat. But she knew it was his gray eyes that set him apart from other handsome men. Devastating eyes that could smolder with desire or light up with amusement or assess a situation at a glance. Tiny flecks of green near his pupils showed when she stood close to him. But those same eyes hid Jake's thoughts as effectively as fog hiding the world from view. And she knew too well how they could become cold steel, filled with determination to get his way.

If she left him, she would be breaking vows that she had

been taught all her life were sacred. The prospect of leaving
him made her feel guilty, but her fears for the future and her
inability to have a baby were stronger.

Her sister thought she'd lost all good sense to walk out on
Jake and the life he could give her. Emily wondered if she
would forever regret leaving him. During the past three weeks
she'd asked herself that question constantly. She knew Jake
wasn't the sort of man to have regrets. He'd move on with his
life—he could find dozens of women who would be thrilled to
take her place. Who could easily give him the family he wanted.

There would be no going back. Jake could be unforgiving.
She had already seen that side of him at work. Strong-willed
and forceful, Jake was accustomed to getting what he wanted.
The evening was going to be difficult. They were on Jake's
turf. If she had waited until they were back at home in Dallas,
this would be a degree easier for her. On his island, he was in
charge. The only way home was to convince Jake to let one
of his planes fly her.

As Jake put his BlackBerry into its holder, his gaze moved
leisurely over her. He approached her, stopping only inches
from her, and slid his hands to her waist. "You look beautiful
and smell wonderful," he said in a husky voice.

"Thank you," she answered solemnly, gazing up at him, her
heartbeat jumping again. She could say the same thing about
him. The scent of his aftershave was faint, yet enticing. The
expression in his eyes curled her toes.

"You'll taste better than any dinner we can find," he added
in a slow drawl that made the temperature in the room climb.
When his gaze lowered to her mouth, she drew a deep breath.
He leaned closer. "You're luscious," he whispered, brushing her
mouth lightly with his. She closed her eyes, placing her hands

on his arms and feeling the solid muscles beneath the elegant suit. Jake drew her to him and covered her lips with his.

The minute his mouth touched hers, her lips parted and his tongue slipped inside, building fires she couldn't control. Knowing she was lost to his kiss, she moaned softly. She wrapped her arms around his neck, pressed against him and returned his kiss.

Her heart drummed. Desire flamed into a scalding inferno that made her cling more tightly as he leaned over her and kissed her passionately.

When at last he released her, it took a second for her to open her eyes. She found him watching her intently. Two emotions showed in his expression—desire and satisfaction. He could always kiss her arguments and complaints into oblivion and he knew it all too well.

"Jake, kisses solve nothing."

"You're right. They start fires that only *you* can put out later," he said in a husky voice. "You're wearing the diamond I gave you. I'm glad you like it," he said.

"It's lovely," she answered.

"Before we go, there's one thing that will make the evening better," he said. Still watching her intently, he reached up to unfasten the tiny ebony buttons, starting at her collar and working his way down. "You have enticing curves that you hide from me even now that we're married."

She wanted to unbutton his shirt, run her hands over his sculpted chest and kiss him again. So easily, he could kiss her into forgetting dinner and their evening plans. She knew she had to keep her hands to herself or she'd never get his attention on conversation. If they made love, instead, she'd be hopelessly sidetracked. Yet it was a struggle to stand quietly while he steadily unfastened button after button. She caught his wrist and held him lightly.

"That's far enough, Jake," she said.

"One more. Let me enjoy the view. Two more until we get off the plane."

Smiling at him, she was unable to refuse. He unfastened three more and pushed the dress open slightly to create a wider V. His fingers drifted lightly over the curves he revealed, making her insides tighten.

"There. I think you look delectable," he said.

"And you're quite irresistible," she told him frankly, wondering if he realized how much she meant what she said.

"I hope so," he answered solemnly, gazing into her eyes with another one of his inscrutable looks. "Shall we go?" he asked. In his usual take-charge manner, he took her arm and headed outside without waiting for her answer. He held the door to his low-slung convertible sports car.

She'd been surprised to learn that Jake had a fleet of fancy cars, which he kept at his various houses. She sat on the soft leather and watched him stride around the car and slide into the seat beside her. As he did, she fastened the three buttons of her dress that he had just opened.

In minutes they were at his private airstrip where his jet was ready and waiting. Toby Uride, his chauffeur, and Brick Prentiss, his bodyguard, were also there. It had taken her a while to get accustomed to all the people who worked for Jake, particularly the bodyguard.

Shortly they were airborne, flying over his island and then the deep blue Caribbean. She spotted Jake's yacht at anchor near the island dock. Farther out, they flew over a sparkling white cruise ship that looked only slightly larger than Jake's yacht.

When she turned, she found him watching her. "You're beautiful, Em," he said, leaning forward to take her hand and run his thumb over her knuckles. She inhaled. With only a look and a slight touch, he made her want him.

"Thank you," she replied, knowing he could hear the breathlessness in her voice.

"That's another facet to you that I like. You always respond to me," he said softly. "I react to you, you know. More than you realize. And you're not always trying to evoke a response. Like now, you're not doing anything, yet you're turning me on."

"If you'd sit back, stop touching and flirting, neither one of us would be so stirred up," she said. She was aware she sounded prim, but she didn't care. "Tonight, all I want is a chance to talk to you without distractions. I want you to listen."

He nodded. "I'll pay attention to whatever you tell me. But I'd rather 'stir you up'. Go right ahead and get me aroused. Making love when we get home will be even better."

His scalding gaze and husky voice were as tantalizing as his touch. She hoped he had no idea what he was doing to her, although she suspected he knew full well. She pulled her hand away and leaned to look out the window again. "This is beautiful, Jake. You should look."

"I am looking," he drawled.

She kept her attention outside, because although her pulse raced, she didn't want him to know how hot and aroused she'd become.

It was a quick flight. Then, with Toby at the wheel of the limousine and Brick in the passenger seat beside him, they drove to one of Jake's friend's luxury hotels. They arrived at an elegant restaurant on the top floor with maroon-and-white decor, and the maître d' addressed Jake by name before leading them to a secluded corner. Seated at a linen-covered table centered with a white candle, they had a panoramic view of flaming torches lighting the beach and, directly below, landscaped grounds with tall palms.

She had iced tea while Jake ordered wine. As soon as they were alone, Jake turned his attention to her again, taking her hand. His fingers were warm. Even that slight contact was electric.

If only she could get pregnant! The longing came daily, and she reminded herself to stop wishing for the impossible. They'd seen the best doctors, made love all the time, and still no baby.

She knew she should be happy with what she had. Jake was sexy and thoughtful. She had an easy, luxurious life, but she wanted more. He was totally engrossed in his achievements. When she'd married him, she'd known that he coveted success, but hadn't realized the full extent of his preoccupation with money, luxury and absolute power.

Candlelight flickered, highlighting Jake's prominent cheekbones, throwing the planes of his face into shadow. She resisted the urge to reach across the table and touch a stray lock of black hair that waved slightly on his forehead. He'd chosen a seductive setting and turned his full attention on her. She had married a charmer deluxe and it was difficult to try to talk about subjects he didn't care to discuss.

In spite of his optimism about their future, she hadn't been able to give him a child. That was why she needed to set him free and let him find a woman who could.

He tilted up her chin. "No long faces," he ordered gently.

"We'll have a baby. All the doctors have said we would. Give us time, Em."

"You've always gotten everything you've wanted."

"Not everything," he said with that steely gaze coming. "Not until I had money and power. Growing up was a whole different story. My dad was a drifter and was killed in a bar-room brawl. Mom had nothing, but she wanted the best for me and my kid sister. Mom always tried to see to it that I had good grades in school, and later, she and I both saw to it that Nina did. My life changed forever when I met Hubert Braden."

She knew about the man who had mentored Jake and his friends, Ryan Warner and Nick Colton.

"It was wonderful that you and your friends got summer jobs landscaping and caring for Hub's property in Dallas, but if you'd never crossed paths with him, I think the three of you would still have made fortunes."

"You have great faith in me," he replied with a smile. "Hub counseled us. Later, after I had my accounting degree, he hired me to work for him and really took me under his wing," Jake said, a faraway look in his eyes. "He gave me financial backing and advice when I went on my own. No, I couldn't have done all this by myself, much less this quickly. I became a billionaire before I was thirty. That's due to his money, influence and the business he tossed my way."

She recalled the frail elderly man who had round-the-clock nursing at his chalet in Switzerland. After their honeymoon, Jake had taken her to meet Hubert Braden. He could barely talk and looked as if he didn't weigh more than eighty pounds. But his eyes lit up at the sight of Jake and she thought Jake's visit with his new bride made him happy.

"You may be right. But as strong-willed and shrewd as you

are, I suspect you would have become a billionaire without help. I don't know why you pursue money to the extent you do. You could live easily on what you have. Why do you want more?"

"I thrive on work. Poverty was hell and I want to be as far away from it as possible. I like making money. Someday I might like to go into politics, and that takes financial backing."

Horrified, she stared at him. "If you say, 'I might like to go into politics,' it translates to 'I might like to run for president.' You don't do anything in a small way."

He laughed. Creases framed his mouth as he revealed his dazzling white teeth. "I'm building a dynasty," he answered, and she heard the steel in his voice. "I hope to have sons to leave it to."

One more reminder that she couldn't give him a baby. She looked away and wondered whether Jake ever thought about the world except on his terms. "That brings us back to what I want to discuss with you," she said stiffly.

"We'll talk soon enough when we won't be interrupted. I see you're all buttoned up again," he added with amusement in his eyes.

"We're in public," she replied. "I'm revealing enough bare flesh. You'll see all you want of me later, I'm sure."

He inhaled deeply. "That thought tempts me to turn around and leave. Of course, we can get a suite here at the hotel. This is one of Ryan's hotels."

"The rich get richer," she replied, wrinkling her nose at him and knowing that he and his close friends still did all sorts of favors for each other as much as they would have if they had been blood brothers.

"Let's dance and see if we can get rid of that solemn look in your big blue eyes." Without waiting for an answer from her, he stood and reached for her hand, giving her one of those looks that could melt her.

Reminding herself to stay firm, she followed him to the dance floor and stepped into his arms as an old ballad played.

He spun her around and dipped low, holding her easily in his strong arms. For a moment she forgot everything as he whirled and leaned over so she had to cling to him. When she gazed up into his eyes, his desire was obvious, making her heart race faster. Breathlessly, she held him as he swung her around, pulling her close.

"That's better," he said, smiling, a warmth in his expression that was like sunshine pouring out when clouds drifted away. She had to smile in return, briefly succumbing to Jake's charisma and letting her worries go.

The ballad ended and a fast number began. Still holding her hand, Jake continued dancing to the faster beat. His muscled body moved with a fit male athlete's grace. Her breasts tingled and with every brush of their bodies—hip against hip, shoulder grazing shoulder—she wanted more of him.

She followed his lead, watching him. Jake's body was long and lean and strong, sexy in his dark suit. She wondered if they would make love when they flew home, or if they would end the evening not even speaking.

While their lovemaking was sensational, there was no intimacy, no real emotion. Tonight, if they made love, would be no different.

When the dance ended, she was hot, breathless. Jake took her arm lightly and they returned to their seats to find their tossed salads waiting.

She took a long drink of ice water, trying to collect herself and stop thinking about Jake's kisses, his hands moving over her. "Tell me about your week," she suggested, setting down the water.

He placed his wineglass on the table. "You're beginning to distract me when I'm away from home. Instead of keeping my mind on business the way I always have, I find myself thinking about you."

"C'mon, Jake. There's no way that I interfere with your thoughts when your mind is on business." She didn't believe him for a minute. Jake could focus on his job with an intensity that amazed her. "I worked for you too long to accept that."

He shrugged, sipped his water and set down the goblet. "Think what you will, but I'm telling the truth. I thought it might flatter you to know. I haven't had this problem with any woman before."

In spite of her certainty that he was exaggerating tremendously, she felt a thrill. She was aware that he knew how to make a woman feel special, and took his compliments lightly. She often wondered if his mind was on business when he said them.

She looked at her successful handsome husband and remembered her decisions earlier in the day. She knew she had to get him back on track and make him listen to her.

"That's very flattering, Jake, but it doesn't change my feelings on our marriage. We've given ourselves time. I'm just not getting pregnant and I know you want a family. You talk about it every time we're together."

"If I'm pressuring you, I'll stop," he said, placing his fork on his plate and looking at her with a direct gaze she met unwaveringly, relieved to finally get his attention.

"No, that's not it. I know having a son is important to you. If I get out of your life, you can find a woman who will give you one." Tears threatened, and she clamped her lips closed and fought to control her emotions.

She didn't want her salad, suddenly, and set down her fork.

He tilted up her chin to study her. "Don't cry," he said gently. "I'm not complaining. I'm not unhappy with you. I don't want to get rid of you or trade you in for a different model. Will you forget all that?"

"I find it difficult to," she replied stiffly, hating that she couldn't control her tears. She wished that he wasn't being so kind.

"Do it, anyway," he ordered, running his index finger lightly over her cheeks to brush away her tears. "Don't cry over something that a year from now may not be an issue between us. The minute you get pregnant, you'll forget all about leaving."

"It isn't just the pregnancy," she said and then bit her lip as their salad plates were removed. She noticed Jake didn't eat all of his salad, either, and she wondered whether he was as calm and self-assured as he acted.

Lobster with melted butter and thick juicy steaks were placed in front of them, and soon they were alone again. Her appetite didn't return as she stared at him. Raven glints in his black hair glowed in the candlelight and his thick eyelashes were dark shadows. Piano music played in the background and Emily knew this moment would be etched in her memory forever.

"You've been great to me," she replied patiently. "You're used to the world on your terms, but this time it isn't conforming."

He reached across the table to touch her cheek, his fingers brushing lightly, yet stirring sparks with the contact. "I promise you that you haven't failed me. I don't want another woman. I don't want to give up on our marriage. It *is* working."

"It's not!" she protested, more strongly than she meant to as she tried to get a grip on her emotions. "I don't care for your materialistic life. You know I'm interested in helping people. You waste so much money. It could be used to make a better life for others. I'm a preacher's daughter and that's the way I've been raised. This isn't my world."

His tolerant smile made her frustration grow. He might as well reach over and pat her on the head, she thought.

"I've given you a generous bank account that I put an abundant amount into each month," he said. "You can spend it however you see fit. I hoped you'd get more clothing, but that's up to you. Even so, you've been doing charity work. You tutor, you've donated your time and money to lots of worthy organizations. But I'm not giving away my fortune. I grew up poor as dirt. I don't want to go back there. We have plenty of places where we're compatible, Em." His voice dropped a notch. "Concentrate on the good things—magic nights, swims in the moonlight, dancing, kissing, making love for hours…"

She drew a deep breath, trying to keep her thoughts on track and knowing how easily he could make her forget her arguments.

"Jake, you're not listening," she said, trying to keep from succumbing to sexy bedroom eyes and a throaty voice. "You're light-years from your former life," she argued. "You've been generous, but you're ambitious and materialistic. I'd prefer a simpler life. You have houses all over the world, a collection of luxury cars, tailor-made suits that cost thousands. Yet you work like you're on your last dollar. If I did get pregnant, I'd want a husband who's home for his child, who coaches Little League, who reads bedtime stories. You'll never have time," she said, her words spilling out, afraid if she didn't say them quickly, she might never get them said.

Smiling, he took her hand. "Dinner will keep. Let's dance again," he said as if he'd already dismissed everything she'd said.

She stared at him. "Are you hearing a word I'm saying?"

He chuckled. "Of course I am," he said, giving a light tug on her hand. "C'mon. We'll dance and talk."

Exasperated, she went with him. On the small dance floor he folded her in his arms. "Will you stop worrying about our future!" he said, laughing softly and brushing her temple with feathery kisses. "You're stewing about Little League, which is years away at best. When I need to, I'll rearrange my schedule." He leaned back to look at her.

She ran her fingers across her brow and placed her hand on his shoulder again. They were barely moving, holding each other and rocking slightly in time to the slow music. "I knew this wouldn't be easy," she said. "Marriage wasn't really meant to be just a convenience for people. Love should be there. Our marriage is sterile in more ways than one."

"You're complaining about my lovemaking?" he asked, his eyebrows arching.

"Of course not!" she replied, feeling her cheeks flush with heat. "No woman could ever complain about your lovemaking," she replied emphatically. "You know what you do to me." Her face grew hotter. "You're one of the sexiest men in the world."

"Ahh! Better! Thank goodness for that," he remarked lightly. "I'll increase the monthly amount I put into your bank account and you can help more people in more ways. How's that?"

"That isn't it at all. Listen to me," she demanded, and took a deep breath. "I want love."

"You didn't when we talked about this before our wedding," he replied with a slight frown. "We were both burned out on relationships and you said this marriage would give us both what we want."

"I know I did, but I was wrong. A spark is missing. Not in the bedroom. In the relationship."

"I haven't been attentive?"

"Yes, Jake. You're attentive and sexy, handsome, charming—"

"You expect me to walk out of your life after you tell me that?" he asked in a husky voice, leaning back to look at her. "If I'm all that to you, then stop worrying, darlin'. Life will fall into place," he said. "If I've got all those qualities and we're compatible—which we are—then love will come in time."

"How can you be so certain?" she exclaimed in annoyance. It was impossible to get him to hear what he didn't want to hear.

The dance ended and he took her hand. While they ate, he told her stories about his week away. She wondered when he stopped work long enough for anything else to happen to him. Or did he make the stories up to get her to laugh? After a time, he glanced at her half-eaten dinner.

"Wasn't your lobster good?"

"It was wonderful, but I'm not that hungry."

"Then let's go home and have a moonlight swim," he said, motioning for their waiter.

Jake continued to be his charming self all through the flight back to the island and the drive to the villa.

The minute they were in the living room, Emily turned to face him. He unfastened a button on his shirt as he moved around, and desire stirred. Jake was so sure of himself that it showed in every move he made. Should she just put aside her worries and accept their life? But she'd been doing that for too long.

"I don't want to swim. I want to talk to you and I want you

to listen. I've tried all evening to tell you. I can't go on with this. I've failed you. And while you say you don't care now, the time will come when you will. Meanwhile, I'm keeping you from becoming a father. I want out of this marriage."

Frowning slightly, he shed his jacket, tossed aside his tie and keys and crossed the room to place his hands on her shoulders. His gaze bore into hers and she took a deep breath.

"I don't want you to go, Em," he said softly, his voice husky and coaxing, the same intimate tone he had when they made love. "I don't want to find another woman. I think this marriage of ours can work. Remember how happy we were the first few months? We can get that back."

His words thrilled her, but they also tore at her. If only she could shove aside her doubts and accept the life Jake wanted to give her!

"You're too materialistic. Money and success are too important to you. We're poles apart in what we want out of life," she argued, struggling to maintain control of her emotions. "Jake, I just can't go on like this."

Something flickered in the depths of his eyes and a muscle worked in his jaw. Otherwise, he looked calm and relaxed as he shook his head.

"At least give us another six months together."

"You're just putting off the inevitable. Six months from now we'll be having this same conversation," she said with a sinking feeling. "I've thought it over constantly, and I don't want to go on with this sham of a marriage. Six months won't matter."

"Maybe, maybe not," Jake replied, gazing at her with speculation obvious in his expression. "I really want you, Em. I don't want to lose you. You're becoming important to me and I think we have a chance for love if you'll just let it happen.

Stop worrying about the future. I want you here with me as my wife. You took vows," he reminded her solemnly.

Hot tears filled her eyes.

"Em, if you'll stay married to me for six more months, I'll give you half a million dollars to use however you want for charity. Give us that six months together to see what will happen. Our marriage is worth a six-month trial. And with half a million dollars, you can do all kinds of charity projects. Is that too much to ask?"

# Two

Emily was stunned by his offer. She stared at him as silence descended. "Six months and half a million dollars?" she asked, amazed that he wanted her so much. She had no idea Jake cared that much about her or their marriage.

His offer meant he wasn't unhappy she hadn't given him an heir. He really wanted to give their marriage a chance. Until now she'd brushed aside all Jake's compliments. For the first time since proposing, she had a faint glimmer of hope that he wanted her as more than a playmate in his bed.

She was shocked that their marriage was so important to him. "You'd give me a half a million dollars for charity? You want me to stay that badly? You're not unhappy with our marriage?" she repeated, feeling weak in the knees. Her head buzzed. The possibility that he truly wanted her to stay longer was stunning, and she could only stare at him.

"I want this marriage to work," he replied coolly, caressing the nape of her neck and consuming her with his gaze. His meandering fingers sent shivers down her spine, which distracted her and reinforced his invitation. "I don't like failure," he said softly, leaning down to brush her ear with a kiss. His warm breath added more fuel to Jake's urging—he was using unfair tactics to get his way, yet she couldn't ignore them.

"I think we have sound beginnings for a solid, satisfying union, so I'm willing to give you an inducement to stay and give us more of a chance," he whispered, showering kisses on her temple, ear and throat. He straightened to look at her and placed his warm hands on her shoulders.

"Half a million—however I want to use it?" she asked, still stunned.

"Yes. It's yours with no strings. Buy clothes with it if you want," he replied with a shrug. He toyed with a lock of her hair, winding it in his fingers. She felt the faint tugs on her scalp.

He sounded relaxed, but his gaze was intense and a muscle worked in his jaw. "Help those kids you work with in that mentoring program. Give it to the children's shelter you support. It's yours."

Warmth and joy poured over her. "Jake, this marriage *is* important to you," she said, flustered by his magnanimous offer, tears of relief stinging her eyes as she hugged him. "I was so sure you really wished you'd never gotten into it. There are so many beautiful women you could have had! I had no idea you really weren't unhappy!" she exclaimed, joy bubbling in her. Worries and stress vanished, replaced by eagerness.

"I think we're going to have a damn good marriage," he declared. "Otherwise, I wouldn't make this offer. With this kind of money you can help others beyond anything you ever envisioned," he said, combing a tendril of brown hair away from her face and smiling at her.

"Keep your money, Jake." The important thing was that he had hope for their marriage. "I'm thrilled. Relieved. The future does look bright!" she exclaimed, excitement making her bubbly.

"I think we have every potential for success. I don't want to lose you. I'm putting the money into your account, but I'm gratified that our marriage is what's so important. You think I'll miss the half a million?" he asked with amusement.

She inhaled deeply. "I wasn't sure how you felt and couldn't imagine that you were happy with me. It's a generous offer, but what changes everything is that you want me to stay and make all this work. I really meant it when I said that you don't have to give me the money," she said, winding her fingers into his hair and realizing she'd misjudged him all this time. Maybe he wasn't as materialistic as she thought. She saw the satisfaction in his expression.

"The money's yours," he replied with a smile. "Just stay with me, Em. We'll be great together," he said, leaning down to cover her mouth with his in a long deep kiss. She threw herself into the kiss, clinging to his lean muscled frame, seeing hope for their future, after all.

"The doctor told you that you were stressed out over not getting pregnant. That's why I took some time off and we came out here for another honeymoon," Jake reminded her, his voice lowering seductively. "For six more months, just relax and take life as it comes, darlin'."

Heat flushed her cheeks when she remembered their first week on the island, when he had taken time off work to stay with her. They had made love constantly and she'd expected to get pregnant, but that had been three weeks ago and she knew she wasn't expecting a baby. "I'm thrilled you want me that badly," she admitted.

He smiled as he gazed warmly down at her. Creases framed his mouth and again he looked his most appealing. "I'm patient and you're anxious. I'm not disappointed, Em. This has been a great bargain. And you won't regret your decision. You can't possibly. You can do good deeds to your heart's content. As far as being 'poles apart' as you said we are, thank heavens. It's more interesting that we're not alike. I don't want to marry someone like me." His voice dropped while he talked and his gaze lowered to her mouth and she forgot about the future and the money.

"This is one thing we have that's special," he whispered. "The lovemaking is fabulous." He lowered his head. His mouth brushed hers and as her insides heated, she had to agree with him.

His mouth opened hers and his tongue went deep, ending all talk as effectively as his half-a-million-dollar offer had. She slid her arms around his neck and pressed against him, kissing him in return as she combed her fingers into his hair.

She stroked his tongue with hers, tasting him, teasing, dimly hearing his groan over the thumping of her heart. It was paradise to be in his arms, to have hope and to be able to finally let go. She wanted to devour him, consume him, give herself completely to him and pleasure him the way he did her.

She twisted her hand in his shirt at the small of his back and pulled, tugging it free of his trousers. Then she ran her hand over his smooth back, wanting to feel all of him. As their kisses grew hotter, he slid his hand down her back slowly, lightly over her bottom and then back up to twist free the tiny buttons of her dress and push away the wisp of lace. He cupped her breast in his hand, his thumb stroking her nipple.

She gasped with pleasure, pressing her hips more tightly against him, kissing him until she pushed lightly against his chest. She hoped to draw this out, to play and pleasure him. She intended to love him for hours. She looked up at him, gasping for breath.

"Let's swim first," she said, gulping to catch her breath. "Let's make this evening last, Jake," she whispered.

"Sure," he said in a husky voice, desire now a steady blaze in his eyes.

"I'm going to our room to get my suit. The one I want isn't in the cabana. I bought a new suit."

"Want me to help you change?" he asked, and she shook her head, smiling at him.

"You meet me at the pool," she said.

"I can't wait," he drawled, touching the end of her nose lightly.

Laughing, she left him, shimmying out of the top of her dress as she crossed the room. It fell around her waist, leaving her bare except for a wisp of a bra.

"Dammit, Em," she heard him mutter, and she turned, slanting a sultry smile at him.

"I'll hurry, Jake," she promised breathlessly and dashed away as he started toward her.

Laughing and eager, she raced upstairs. Her heart throbbed with desire and joy and she wondered if she was going to fall in love with her handsome husband, after all.

Six more months with Jake! He truly wanted her. This marriage wasn't such a cut-and-dried bargain, after all!

The knowledge had lifted an enormous burden off her shoulders. And maybe it would help with getting pregnant. Dr. Claywood had assured her that she *could* get pregnant. He'd told her to relax and given her a list of books to read on the subject.

Plus she had a half a million to spend as she pleased! Emily could think of projects at her father's church—a remedial reading program for kids and one for adults. Mission trips to help rebuild old churches. Free breakfasts for the needy. There were countless places where the money would help. She was on the board of a children's shelter and worked with a mentoring program. The money was fabulous and she was grateful to Jake for his generosity, yet she wished he would do more things on his own to help others. She shrugged away her concern, thankful for what he'd done already.

In their bedroom she hurried to change to a new black two-piece swimsuit. It was skimpy, but she planned to wear it only on occasions when she was alone with Jake. Although, she knew she didn't really need to go to any effort to turn him on. A look, a caress or a kiss could do that. It amazed her how easily he became aroused.

She strolled to the end of the natural rock pool as he swam up, shaking his head and raking his raven hair back away from his face. Smiling, she unfastened her coverup and took her time taking it off, knowing he was watching her, tingling beneath his steamy gaze. He floated at the edge of the pool, his arms crossed on the rocks.

She walked close to the edge and struck a pose, her hand on her hip. "Like my suit?" she asked in a sultry voice, turning first one way and then another. He looked her over and his gray eyes held scalding desire.

"Fabulous," he said in a deep voice.

"I bought it for you," she replied.

"Come here, Em," he said in a throaty rasp that strummed her nerves.

She hurried a few feet away from him and jumped in, surfacing with her head tilted back to get her hair out of her face. Hands closed on her waist.

"I like your suit," he said, running his hands over her hips as they both treaded water. She drew a deep breath. His hands slipped lightly across her breasts, a faint touch, yet scalding. As she drew closer, her leg slid between his and she felt his arousal.

"I thought all this cold water would keep you cooled down."

"Not when you look like that," he said, staring at her mouth. She ran her hands over his broad shoulders, relishing the hard muscles. She wanted to touch him everywhere, needed bare skin against bare skin.

Jake's mouth covered hers. Her awareness splintered among his kiss, the cold water swirling around her and his warm body against her, his leg between hers, pressing intimately. Holding her tightly with one arm around her waist, he let his other hand drift down her bare back over the tiny string that held her top in place. His kiss went deep, distracting her so that she was only dimly aware of his hands moving over her, tossing aside the top of her suit and then peeling away the bottom, his hand caressing the inside of her thigh. Sensations tangled, melting together, fueling fires already raging.

Her moan was both pleasure and need. His hands cupped her breasts, thumbs circling her nipples while she cried out in pleasure.

"Let's get out of the pool," he said gruffly, hoisting himself out and then leaning down to pull her into his arms.

His black suit molded to his amply endowed male body. She peeled it away to free him. Wanting him desperately, she ran her hands along his muscled thighs and then over his tight bottom. He kissed her and walked her backward, his legs against hers until her calves bumped a chaise longue.

He'd been gone a week, and she'd been alone. He was a passionate lover and she was eager for his powerful male body, his bone-melting kisses.

Jake cupped her breasts in his warm hands, dark against her pale skin.

"You're beautiful! You have a gorgeous body." He leaned down to take her nipple in his mouth, his tongue curling around it, stroking it. She clung to his broad shoulders and closed her eyes, moaning with pleasure. She ran her hands over him, needing to caress and stir him to frenzied heights the way he was doing to her so easily.

Jake picked her up and placed her on the chaise, sitting beside her and showering kisses over her breasts as his hands roamed freely over her.

Gasping and writhing with pleasure, she trailed her hands down over his chest, tangling in damp chest hair, then sliding to a washboard stomach. She heard him inhale deeply as he kissed her throat, trailing lower to kiss her breast. He teased her, nibbling and licking and then showering kisses across her stomach while his hand stroked the inside of her thighs.

With a cry of need, she turned him to rub her breasts against his back, wanting his hard, lean body against her. Tonight, passion carried more emotion than any time they had ever made love. Hope for their future and a knowledge that he wanted her both fueled her need for him. She ran her hand over his flat stomach to his thick hard erection and wrapped her hand around it.

He inhaled sharply and turned to kiss her hungrily. Then she was on her back again. Jake's mouth and hands explored every inch of her until he buried his head between her thighs and teased with his tongue, a torment that fanned blazes.

She tangled her hands in his hair, spreading her legs and arching against him. Emily cried out with pleasure, wanting him inside her, wanting him more than ever before.

Tension built like a spring coiling tighter and tighter, sweeping her into a whirlwind. "Jake!" she cried out, raising her head to bite his shoulder. She dug her nails into his back, then scrambled around to take his thick rod in her mouth, running her tongue over the velvet tip.

Now his hands were tight fists in her hair while he licked her. His tongue toyed with her even as she teased him. With a groan, he flipped them so that she was on her back with Jake's weight on her. He kissed her hard, pinning her to the chaise while she writhed beneath him.

He knelt and spread her legs, watching her, leaning down to enter her slowly. He filled her and paused, driving her wild with need, and then withdrew. She screamed his name and tugged at him, wrapping her long legs around his waist and pulling at his bottom as she arched up to meet him.

He thrust hard and fast. Her world spun, blurred. Sensations melted into one driving force, all consuming as she rose toward the brink. The tension became unbearably exquisite.

His control vanished and he plunged fast, sending her over the edge. Ecstasy burst in bright lights behind her closed eyelids and her pulse drummed in her ears. Dimly she felt him shudder as he pumped his release in her. She clung tightly to his virile body, rocking with him.

Their ragged breathing became quiet. Sated, they held each other tightly. She hoped a baby would come from their lovemaking. Emily rubbed her temple against his warm shoulder.

Tonight she had hope and, for the first time, a sense that Jake wanted her. She marveled at these new discoveries, relishing them like newfound treasure. Their marriage might indeed blossom into love.

When he turned them on their sides, she was still enveloped in his embrace. He stroked her back and brushed tendrils of hair from her face. "You're fantastic, Em."

"You stole my line. What a lover you are, Jake. And tonight was so very special. I can't tell you how happy you've made me and how much hope for our future I have now."

He held her close, his voice a deep rumble. "Good. That makes me happy, too. This is what we needed, Em. A clearer understanding. I want you as my wife. You're important to me."

"Jake." She sighed with pleasure and turned her head to kiss him. A long scalding kiss that made him groan.

She lay her head against his chest. "Jake, this is the best night of our marriage."

"I quite agree," he said. "You have a fantastic body. You keep it hidden beneath those clothes you wear."

"I'm sure you would've enjoyed having a secretary who wore skintight revealing clothes."

"Yes, I might have. Particularly if she was as efficient and competent as you."

"Thank you," she said, pleased by the compliment.

"See, I told you that love will bloom," he said with satisfaction. "I think it's pretty damn good between us right now," he added, smiling at her.

"Tonight *has* been special. I'll remember it all my life. And I hope you're right about love for both of us." She stroked his chest. "Have you ever really been in love?"

"No," he said, his smoky eyes hiding his true thoughts.

"Not really. I've had relationships and some were longer than others and better than others, but I've never been deeply in love. I've never felt fireworks, never wanted any woman with me for the rest of my life."

For just a moment she was quiet as she thought about that description and wished that someday she would fill it.

"You're marvelous, Em, and our marriage is good—we'll come to love each other."

"You think that because you always expect to get what you want," she reminded him as she traced his jaw with her fingers, feeling the tiny stubble of a beard. Her hand slipped lower, along the strong column of his neck and across one broad shoulder. "Fireworks don't come with familiarity, Jake. Fireworks and a racing heart come from love at first sight. Never with convenience."

"Perhaps. I keep asking you to have patience and faith."

"You've been unbelievably generous," she said, still amazed by his offer. "I'm surprised you don't take a more active role in helping people. Someone helped *you*."

"I will someday," he answered casually. "I give to charities."

"You give money, not time. And never yourself. I'm just surprised that you don't want to get more involved."

"I'm too busy right now. I guess I really never think about it."

"I'll let you know how every dime of your gift is spent and you'll see what good you did."

"Forget that," he answered with amusement in his voice. "I don't need to know about all the projects. I have a more urgent project right now." He pulled her up and leaned closer to kiss her ear while he caressed her nape.

She raised slightly to gaze down at him. "You have an insatiable appetite for sex."

"You bring it out in me," he teased, and she realized this was turning out to be one of the good moments between them. Or had she just finally relaxed and accepted that he did want this marriage, that he still wanted her as his wife?

At the moment she didn't care. Running her fingers lightly over his bare chest, she brushed his lips with a feathery kiss and then rained kisses on his neck.

"Ahh, baby," he said, "that feels good," he continued in a husky voice.

Her hand played over him, drifting lower over his muscled stomach, touching him. He was hard and ready again.

"Jake, you're decadent," she whispered in his ear, tracing the curves of his ear with her tongue.

He rolled her over, settling his weight on top of her as he kissed her passionately, starting fires anew.

Later, they showered together and made love until the early-morning hours, when she fell asleep in his arms.

When she stirred again, she was alone in their bed. It was Friday morning. Sunshine poured through open doors and windows. Upon Jake's return, the servants had been given several days off, so she had the house to herself.

Stretching, she smiled as she thought about the night. It was intimate and they had bonded. Jake had seemed as happy as she. Maybe there actually was a chance for them.

Last night had changed her feelings for him. She wondered about their depth. Was she already falling in love with him? She ran her hand over her stomach, thinking last night had been the most relaxed she'd been with him since the early months of their marriage.

She stepped out of bed, pulling on a white cotton robe. She had wanted to go back to Dallas, but now she was in no hurry.

She wanted to prolong her idyll with Jake. Being with him was fabulous—this was turning into a real second honeymoon.

She thought about his abundant energy—even when relaxed, he seemed to move. Only after long bouts of work or lovemaking did he finally get quiet. The rest of his waking hours he was restless.

She smiled again when she thought about him. She was tempted to call him, but she never disturbed him when he was at work. An old secretarial habit, she was certain.

On the desk she found a note from him saying he had flown to Houston. He would be back tonight in time to take her to dinner. In his scrawling handwriting, she read, "…dinner and seduction again…"

He had underlined "seduction," and she knew he meant it would be another night of lovemaking. Her toes curled when she simply remembered the previous night. Anticipation simmered and she planned a candlelight dinner with Jake's favorite food—steak—and his favorite wine. She tried to think what she could do to make his homecoming as sexy as possible.

Pampering herself, she had a hot bath in their huge marble tub. She finally climbed out, wound a thick green bath towel around her and went to their closet to find something to wear. As she passed Jake's side of the closet, a thick white envelope lying on the floor caught her attention. He must have dropped it or let it fall out of one of his pockets.

She picked up the envelope to place on his chest of drawers, but saw it was addressed in neat feminine handwriting to Mr. and Mrs. Jacob Thorne.

What woman had been writing to both of them? Why hadn't Jake mentioned it if it had been addressed to her, too? She studied the envelope.

Jake hadn't shown it to her. The return address indicated the letter was from Hubert Braden, and she realized his nurse must have written it. Emily studied the envelope further and saw it had arrived over a week ago. Puzzled why Jake hadn't even mentioned it, she decided he had stuffed it into his pocket and forgotten it.

She was curious about the man who had been such a big influence in Jake's life, the father figure he wanted, and she wished now they'd spent more time visiting Mr. Braden. Since the letter was addressed to her, too, she saw no reason not to read it. She withdrew the letter and unfolded it, looking at more of the flowing cursive. Obviously it had been dictated.

Suddenly Emily stiffened, stunned by what she was reading. Jake had some explaining to do.

# Three

Emily's hands shook as she read the letter once more:

Dear Jake and Emily:
How nice it was for both of you to visit an old man. Jake, your bride is beautiful, and I can rest in peace knowing that you are married now and settled down. You are my biggest success. I have one more legacy to leave to you, but as you recall when we talked before your marriage, there are stipulations.

I have a long list of bequests in my will. Some will go to Ryan and Nick, of course. The three of you are like family to me. But I consider *you* the son I never had. I've mentored you and watched you succeed. I want the best for you.

If you and Emily have a baby, or conceive before my

demise, then you will inherit the bulk of my estate. Otherwise, if there is no child, my estate will go to the charities listed below and you will receive the same amount as Ryan and Nick. I hope to see you permanently settled with the same woman. I heartily approve of your choice. Emily seems a fine young woman and I was delighted to see the pictures of both your wedding and the nursery you have ready for your first child.

I'm doing this because I want you to start a family while you are young and strong and can enjoy your children. I know how important work and success are to you, so I feel you need this incentive. Time slips away too easily.

I was too busy for children and consequently spent my last years alone. I'm meddling in your life, but that's all I have left…

Shocked, Emily dropped the letter. She stared into space and saw Jake asking her to marry him and then later, repeating wedding vows to her. His offer to make her stay, his declarations of desire… Now she knew the true reason. He'd done it for money!

He had deceived her from the start! He'd told her he thought it was time he married, but he'd never mentioned that if he married and had a baby, he would inherit another billion dollars or more from his mentor.

"Permanently settled…." The words leaped out at her. No wonder Jake wanted her to stay with him! Half a million was nothing when more than a billion-dollar inheritance was at stake! The enormity of Jake's deception was like a tidal wave hitting her.

How *could* he! He had married her to get Hubert Braden's fortune! The only reason Jake wanted a baby was to make more money. The same went for her, too—he only wanted her to stay so he could claim his inheritance.

Her stomach roiled and she felt sick, running into the bathroom to lose what little dinner she'd eaten the night before. She ran a washcloth under the tap and then wiped her face and her hands with it.

The enormity of his deception stunned her. Their entire relationship was built on lies. She looked at the letter again, skimming over it as if touching a wound— "...delighted to see the pictures of...the nursery you have ready..."

She remembered a very late night in June, two months after their wedding, when she was in Jake's arms and he suggested they get a nursery ready.

"Em, we're trying to start our family. Let's go ahead and furnish a nursery."

She had remained silent so long that he raised himself to look down at her. "Cat got your tongue?" he asked.

She drew her fingers across his chest, relishing the taut muscles. "Jake, I guess it's superstition, but I'm a little leery of getting a nursery ready before I'm pregnant. It's sort of tempting Fate. We'll have almost nine months once I find out I'm pregnant."

His smile was warm, irresistible. He combed long tendrils of hair from her face, stirring faint tingles. "Nonsense!" He nuzzled her cheek and raised his head again. "It'll be fun. Let's get one ready. We both had physicals before we married and were told we could have a family. I want to get the nursery ready now."

"You sound as if you already have a theme in mind," she said, thinking how he had to control every facet of his life.

"Not at all," he answered easily, caressing her throat and letting his hand slide lower. "I'm leaving the design and decor totally up to you. You can run it past me, but I trust your choices."

"If we wait, we'll know whether we're decorating for a girl or boy," she argued, uneasy about establishing a nursery before she was pregnant. Not even Jake's optimism could squelch her fears.

"There are all sorts of appealing themes that would work for either a boy or girl. You'll work that out with a decorator. Money's no object. I'll talk to a contractor and we'll have a door put in the wall that opens to the bedroom next to this one if you want the nursery close to our room."

"Of course I do! I'll probably have a crib in here for a while."

"Maybe," he said, showering light kisses on her throat and muddling her concentration of their discussion. "I'll call a contractor tomorrow and get furniture moved out of that room so when you have a decorator, it'll be ready."

"Jake, this just gives me the most uneasy feeling. I'll worry every time I pass the room."

"Scaredy-cat," he teased. "We'll get it ready, then close the door on it. You don't need to see it or go into it. You can forget it's there."

"Then why have it?"

"To humor me," he answered, brushing kisses lower over her breasts at the edge of the sheet. His breath was warm and her nipples were taut, desire flaring again. She was constantly amazed how easily he could get her aroused, but she was equally surprised how effortlessly she could get Jake hard and ready. Her leg was thrown over him and she could feel his arousal.

"You are so sexy," she whispered, biting his shoulder lightly.

She nuzzled his neck, while her hand slipped beneath the sheet to run over his thigh.

Inhaling deeply, Jake had moved lower with his kisses. She'd felt his hot breath on her nipple through the sheet seconds before he'd pushed the sheet away to kiss her. He'd run his tongue over her taut bud, destroying all conversation.

Staring into space now, Emily reflected on those early months. A kaleidoscope of memories flashed in her mind—Jake constantly asking if she'd hired a decorator or started on the nursery, threatening to do so himself and finally prodding her into picking out a nursery-rhyme theme with characters from the old stories and poems. When the room was finished, she remembered his pleasure—he'd even taken digital pictures of the room. Now she understood why. Those pictures had been e-mailed to Hubert Braden, to convince him that Jake had settled with a wife and they were trying to have a baby.

Did he ever intend to tell her, or was he planning on getting the inheritance and letting her think that Hubert Braden had simply named him his primary heir?

She was certain that Jake would never have admitted his deception. Every kiss was a lie.

Revolted, she shook with rage. She should have known—she knew only too well how driven Jake was, after all. She'd watched him work, seen the drive that allowed no room for failure, seen it consume his time and energy and concentration. Why had she been so naive? She'd known she was dealing with a tiger whose natural instincts were to satisfy himself above all else. Acquiring money was what Jake thrived on.

Hubert Braden probably wouldn't approve of Jake getting a divorce. He'd seemed inordinately pleased by their marriage, and now she understood why Jake was fighting to keep her.

A half a million dollars to stay was an insignificant investment for him, yet he knew it would dazzle her. She wouldn't be able to turn him down. His declarations of affection, his request that she give them a chance to fall in love—all lies!

Tears of anger and frustration streamed down Emily's cheeks. Never in her life had she felt so betrayed and exploited.

Jake the Snake. The nickname fit. Rage blazed in her, growing with every passing minute. She realized now why he'd wanted to marry her in the first place. He must have seen her as the naive secretary, impressed by him. He'd probably thought she'd be so blinded by his money, she'd do whatever he wanted. Jake was calculating and shrewd, and she was certain he'd thought it all out. Society women would make far more monetary demands on him than she would.

She was angry with herself for being so gullible and trusting Jake completely. How dare Jake deceive her! And why did he have to have the inheritance? Why did he want it badly enough to delude her about it? He was already a billionaire— why did he want so much more? She knew he thrived on wealth and he equated money with success. But how greedy was he?

Later, when Jake had Hubert's money, had he planned on dumping her and keeping his child? Or would he get rid of them both? She suspected there were only two things in life Jake truly loved—himself and money. Was he scrambling to be the world's richest man? If he had political ambitions, they had to be presidential. Jake would never settle for anything less than the highest possible office.

Well, he could keep his half million. She was getting out of this marriage. She never wanted to see Jake again.

Unable to remain still, she rushed to the closet for a suitcase. She was getting out of Jake's life and she couldn't go fast enough. Their marriage was over.

Packing furiously, she knew when she walked out of his life, she would leave most everything he'd given her behind. She glanced at the letter and yanked it up. She made the bed, smoothing away every wrinkle in the expensive gold-and-white satin duvet, propping elegant gold-and-white accent pillows across the bed. With care, she placed the letter in the center of the bed where Jake couldn't miss it or its implications.

She suspected Jake would try to hold her to her promise to stay for six more months as his wife. He'd probably include sex in that bargain, too. But she didn't want Jake's baby anymore. Thank heaven she wasn't pregnant.

Or *was* she?

Memories of their lovemaking just hours earlier rose to haunt her. She pressed a palm to her flat tummy, suddenly scared that she might already be carrying his baby. She swayed and closed her eyes, praying that she wasn't. Surely, if she hadn't gotten pregnant in all this time…

"Please," she whispered. "I don't want Jake's baby." They had made love for hours, all through the night. She clamped her mouth shut and prayed again that she wasn't already carrying his baby. She was not going to be a part of Jake winning Hubert Braden's inheritance!

As far as she was concerned, Jake broke their vows when he deceived her. She couldn't get out of this sham marriage soon enough.

Barely aware of her tears, Emily stormed around the room, finding her cell phone. She called one of Jake's pilots and ordered a plane to be readied in three hours. As the pilot stammered and tried to put her off, she tightened her grip on the phone.

"Look, do I have to get Jake to get a plane here for me?" she asked sharply, her patience shredding. "I want to get back to Dallas to my family as soon as possible."

"No, ma'am. I'll be there and ready to go to Dallas by noon," the pilot replied.

"Thank you," she said, and snapped her phone closed. Fury made her pack faster.

Her hands shook as she flung clothes into her suitcase. She looked at the velvet box with the diamond necklace. If she sold it, she could give the money to the church. She grabbed up the jewelry Jake had given her, tossing it into her suitcase, determined to get rid of every glittering bit of it.

Seething with anger, she showered and dressed in beige slacks and a matching shirt, then tied her hair behind her head with a silk scarf. As noon approached, she set her suitcases by the door. While she waited for the driver to come pick her up, she looked around the extravagant villa, remembering time spent with Jake in every part of the house. When he'd been with her, Jake had always been working toward a goal— as surely as if he'd been doing battle in a boardroom.

As she left the villa, she refused to look back. In minutes, she was at Jake's airstrip where a sleek jet was ready and waiting to take her home.

Shortly after twelve, the plane lifted off the island. Still burning with fury, she gazed below at Jake's sprawling villa and the green jewel of an island in the blue sea. When she got home, she'd get a divorce and end this sham marriage. In fact, because of the deceit, she might even be able to have their marriage annulled. She could pretend the whole thing never happened.

She had no place to go in Dallas except her parents' house. But sooner or later, Jake would show up and she wanted to have that confrontation in private and keep her parents out of it. Thanks to Jake she had a hefty savings account. She toyed with the idea of going to Fort Worth or Houston or even out of state and letting Jake search for her to give herself some time before she faced him. But in the end that was just postponing the inevitable.

The prospect of working in Dallas where they might occasionally cross paths didn't appeal to her. But when she considered moving away, she felt deflated. Her family and friends were all in Dallas. While she was certain she could make new friends, she didn't want to sever close ties. Dallas was big enough that she and Jake might never see each other.

She vowed she wouldn't trust Jake again. He'd deceived her because she'd been gullible and trusting. Never again would she accept anything Jake said without questioning his motives. He was driven and power-grubbing. His world revolved around himself and she needed to remember that.

When she landed in midafternoon, she took a taxi to a hotel and booked a suite. Next, she went to their house to get her car, pack her things and move what she needed to the hotel.

She spent the next few hours mulling over plans. Next week she would find a lawyer and see about getting an annulment or a divorce. She wondered if she'd have a difficult time finding an attorney who would fight with Jake's battery of brilliant, successful lawyers. And with a billion-dollar inheritance at stake, Jake would definitely fight.

Well, he had chosen the wrong woman. Her first instincts had been right. That first night when he had proposed a marriage of convenience, she should have stuck with her initial reaction—that it was preposterous and would never work. How right she had been!

Jake always trusted his instincts. She should have trusted her own.

Soon she would have to see about a job. This would mean giving up her charity work, changing her lifestyle yet again. It occurred to her that she could make Jake pay for what he'd done, but then she dismissed the notion. She just wanted him out of her life.

She'd have to give up some things if she got a job. She co-ordinated tutors to help students in the elementary grades with reading, math and language. She volunteered two afternoons a week at a school where she met with the tutors, talking to them briefly and answering their questions, then spending one-on-one time with anyone who needed it.

She also served on the board of a children's shelter. But it took up a lot of her time, so that would have to go.

She could continue tutoring a child in math and science on Wednesday evenings at her father's church. She'd become friendly with four young men who were on a high-school football team. They gave an hour one night a week to mentor elementary kids. She could continue to help them with that. Gradually she was getting to know both the younger students and their tutors, and her heart went out to all of them. The contrast between their lives and Jake's disturbed her.

The Dallas hotel she'd checked into was on a busy highway, but she was in a suite that faced away from the highway and overlooked the pool. She charged the suite to Jake. She didn't care if he knew.

She had a balcony with a table and chairs. The decor of her living area was beige and white and very elegant. She knew soon she'd get used to a more modest style of living and save her money, but she didn't plan to be in the hotel long. She had enough in her savings account for a down payment on a condo. With Jake's money, she could take her time to look for a job and a place to live.

She ordered dinner through room service and as night fell, she was surprised she hadn't heard from Jake. He should have returned to the island by now.

At ten o'clock her cell phone rang, and she answered to hear Jake's deep voice.

"I'm in the hotel. I'm coming up to see you," he said with a note of steel in his voice.

"Fine," she replied, realizing that sooner or later, she would have to talk to him and she might as well get it over with. With a click of the phone, Jake was gone. He'd found her sooner than she'd expected, but he had endless resources at his disposal. She put away her phone and stepped in front of a mirror. Her hair fell free across her shoulders. She wore a red silk blouse and matching slacks. Satisfied with her looks, she waited for his knock.

"Emily, it's Jake," he said in a low voice. She opened the door and he came striding into the room, as dynamic a presence as ever. His commanding gaze stabbed into her.

He was still in his suit, but his tie was gone and his shirt was unbuttoned at the throat. Locks of his black hair fell slightly on his forehead as if tangled by the wind. He towered over her. In his expensive flawless suit, he looked commanding. Pulling the letter out of his pocket, he held it out. "I suppose this is why you left."

"Yes. I want a divorce," she said. She tried to keep her voice civil, but her fists were clenched and she was trembling with anger again. "How could you deceive me the way you did?" she blurted out, unable to control her fury.

In agitation, she crossed the room to put some distance between them and then whirled to face him. "You married me to get Hubert's money. Not for any other reason!" she snapped. "I hate you, Jake, for your duplicity."

A muscle worked in his jaw, but otherwise he looked calm. "I think you're making a mountain out of a molehill. We married because it was convenient, not for love. I never told you I loved you."

"A molehill!" She struggled to get her voice back down. "Your greed is astounding. You'll do anything for money! Why didn't you just tell me what the deal was and let me decide if I wanted to get married under those circumstances?"

"You know you wouldn't have."

"If you think I wouldn't have, then you know full well that you were doing something underhanded and wrong! I can't believe how conniving you are!" She was hot with anger and her voice had risen. She hated his unshakable cool demeanor.

"All right, maybe I should have told you. But that's over and done. Now that you know, why can't we go on with this marriage? You'll still get all sorts of things you never would have otherwise. And if we split up, you may never get married again. You might never have those children you want," he stated flatly. "You're thirty-one now," he reminded her. "Your biological clock is ticking."

"You needn't remind me," she replied stiffly, hating him with her whole being. "I don't want my children to have a father who loves money more than anything else on earth. And last night…that was the most devious behavior of all. You led me to believe that you cared, that there was a chance for our marriage to be real. That love would come. 'I told you that

love will bloom,' you said. 'I want this marriage to work,'"
she quoted. "'I think this marriage has every potential for success. I don't want to lose you.'" She glared at him. "It was lie
upon lie," she added, not caring about his excuses.

"You're blowing this all out of proportion, Emily. And
we've been good together. Deny *that* one," he said, leveling
a look at her that only increased her fury.

"What else haven't you told me? What other big shocks
lie in store?"

"That's it," he snapped, for the first time scowling at her.
"That inheritance changes nothing between you and me."

"It changes everything. You weren't straightforward with
me. It's a betrayal of my trust!"

He pushed open his jacket to place his hands on his hips.
He stared at her, his gray eyes glacial. "It's ridiculous for you
to waste your money staying at this hotel. Come out to the
house. You can stay down the hall and we can avoid each other
as much as you want, but we can talk things over and come
to some agreement."

"I'm not moving in with you," she said. Was he listening
to her at all? "I want a divorce. Or an annulment. Now I know
why you fought the idea of divorce so strongly. Evidently,
Hubert will cut you out of that inheritance if you divorce."

"He hasn't said that in so many words," Jake said, but his
face flushed, and she suspected she was exactly right.

"And the nursery, Jake. I see why you wanted a nursery.
I'm sure you sent pictures of it to Hubert," she said and saw
Jake's face flush even more. For once, he couldn't maintain
his impassive gaze. "You didn't give a fig for the nursery! You
may not even care about the baby if you ever have one. You're
after money."

"I wanted him to know we were planning a family."

"Of course you did. The only reason you haven't lied to him and told him I'm pregnant is because you know he'll want to meet the baby or see pictures. Well, you married the wrong woman," she said. "I want out of this marriage." She raised her chin. She wondered if Jake had ever been told he was going to have to do something he didn't want to do.

His eyes narrowed. "You promised just a little over twenty-four hours ago that you would give me another six months. You gave me your word. And I agreed to give you a half a million dollars."

"You're a fine one to talk about giving your word!" she cried, winding her fingers together tightly.

"You promised me, Emily. Six more months." He rubbed the back of his neck and gave her a stormy look. "You're giving up a half a million dollars' worth of help for all those people you say need it so desperately."

"I'm not letting you touch me again. I don't want to have your baby! I don't want to get pregnant by you. My body is mine—you can never buy it. Never!"

"*Never* is a hell of a long time and you have a lot to learn about negotiation," he said imperturbably, fueling her anger.

"You don't deserve to have me honor my promise."

"Perhaps not," he said, leveling a cold hard look at her. "But you won't be able to live with yourself if you don't honor what you promised. It doesn't matter one damn bit what I did when it comes to you giving your word. You live by a code of honesty and you know you're going to have to uphold it to feel good about yourself."

Suspecting he was right, she frowned. "This is one time I'll live with guilt. I'm not coming back with you. I don't want more intimate moments with you or to help you get more money. You're consumed with greed, Jake!"

"You haven't disliked intimate moments with me in the past," he reminded her. She glared at him in silence, seeing they were at an impasse.

"This marriage is finished," she declared.

"Maybe," he said, studying her. "I'm always open to negotiation, Emily. You need to learn to salvage what you can from a bad situation," he said.

"There's nothing I want to salvage here. Deceitfulness is unforgivable. I can't trust you."

He shrugged, dismissing her. He jammed his hand in his pocket and gazed at her with speculation. Another lock of black hair curved over his forehead, giving him a slightly disheveled appearance that was usually enticing. She had no idea what he was thinking, but she was certain he was trying to figure out a way to talk her into doing what he wanted. She folded her hands across her middle and stared at him. She could wait as long as he could—she had no intention of letting him talk her into staying.

"Now think before you answer. Use your head and not your emotions."

"I'll really try, Jake," she said with sarcasm.

"You stay…"

She opened her mouth to protest and he held up his hand, giving her a warning look.

"Hear me out before you answer. Always listen to the offer and weigh your options. You stay the six months with me at my Dallas home, stay as my wife—"

"Absolutely not!"

"Listen to me. Stay married to me in name only—a true

paper marriage of convenience this time—for the six months and I'll increase that half million I'm giving you to one million. That's one million dollars for you, your family, your charities, whatever you want to spend it on. You can never do that much good for people, Emily, if you say no and walk out now."

Once again, Jake had shocked her. She drew a deep breath. In spite of her protests and her fury, she knew that she had to think this over. That was too much money to blow off for her own selfish reasons. And he knew it. Nothing changed in his expression, but she was certain that Jake expected her to accept.

She stared at him, hoping she seemed as unruffled as he. "Well, maybe I can learn something about negotiation from the master, Jake. I want tonight to think over your offer."

He nodded. "Fair enough," he replied with a note of confidence. "Sleep on it and think about what you'd be giving up. A million dollars is a helluva lot of money." He turned slightly as if to leave, but then paused. "I'll come here in the morning—half-past seven. You can give me your answer. If you stay, I'll take you to breakfast. If you don't, I'll go on my way."

She doubted he would do any such thing without another battle, but she nodded. "Agreed. I'll see you in the morning."

He gave her a long searching look and then turned and left. She let out her breath, shaking now that Jake had gone. It had taken a toll to match wits with him and try to stay as calm as he was. Her hands were clammy and her stomach churned. She'd wanted to throw something at him, smash something against the door he'd just walked through.

She rushed to switch off the lights and stepped out onto the balcony into the chilly Dallas night. She sat in a chair and watched the traffic below, remembering she hadn't eaten all day. But she didn't care. She felt like even one bite of food would make her gag.

Below, she saw half of a limo parked on the hotel drive, the rest of it hidden by the portico. It was Jake's—she saw Toby leaning against it, waiting patiently for Jake to come out.

Then she saw Jake emerge from under the portico and stride across the driveway, his long legs eating up the distance to the limo. Wind tangled locks of his hair. A doorman on the driveway moved out of his way and a car halted to let him cross. She watched him climb into the limo and the chauffeur close the door. In seconds the limo pulled out and disappeared around the curve of the hotel driveway.

She went inside, closing the door. But she still felt Jake's domineering presence in the empty room.

While she pondered her options, she sat inside by a window to look out at the traffic.

Why would he offer her marriage in name only? That wouldn't get him the baby he wanted. She knew Jake had a reason for everything he did. He was probably certain if he could keep her under his roof, he could seduce her. And he could still tell Hubert about his wife at home. She knew that on Jake's European jaunts, he often called on his mentor.

She thought of the children who were being tutored and all they needed. The four high-school football players who mentored the elementary kids could use some new supplies, too. One of the high-school boys, Orlando Crane, seemed talented and bright, but because of difficulties at home trying to take care of his siblings, he could barely stay in school himself. Their high school was the poorest in the system. The team only had tattered faded uniforms and poor equipment. She could use the money in so many ways. Jake had made her an offer she had to consider. What was she going to do?

Jake gazed unseeingly out the window of the limo. "Dammit!" he swore, thinking about the letter. That letter from Hub he should've tossed.

It had been sent to his office and he'd stuck it into his pocket to read on the way to a meeting. He'd meant to shred it when he returned to the office. Instead, he had forgotten about it.

He thought about making love with Emily. She set him on fire. Last night, she was the most passionate she'd ever been, willing to do anything, eager and responsive. He slow-played memories of later, standing in front of the mirror where he could watch her while he fondled and caressed her, demolished all her control. Hot and aroused now, he shifted uncomfortably. He'd spent all day looking forward to tonight. He'd expected another night of passion—only to discover she wanted a divorce.

She surprised him. She had been composed and calm tonight. No tears, no screaming. But then he'd known for a long time that she was intelligent. For a moment he wondered why in the hell he hadn't just married some gorgeous babe who loved cars and diamonds and wouldn't have given him a moment's trouble. But then he knew he would have been bored in six months. So far, he couldn't claim one minute of boredom with Emily.

She'd looked beautiful, too—willowy, curvaceous, luscious. He drew a deep breath, thinking about when he'd opened the door and she'd been standing there, fire in her blue eyes. The red silk clung to her curves without flaunting them in his face. Just seeing her had ignited fires at a time he couldn't handle a blaze.

He didn't think he could be angry and frustrated and aroused at the same time, but tonight he'd learned that he could. His first inclination had been to cross the room, take her into his arms and kiss away all her objections. For once, she had a wall of resistance between them as hard as a slab of concrete.

If she accepted his offer—and he expected her to—he'd have her under his roof and if so, it was only a matter of time until he could seduce her. And he would still be able to talk to Hub about her being with him. Jake inhaled deeply, clenching his fist. If only he'd gotten Em pregnant last night. Maybe he had. For if she got pregnant, it would solve everything—give her something to occupy her mind and her time besides the damnable charities.

Just remembering the previous night heated him. She'd felt so smooth, so satiny in his arms, and her curves were so delectable. He remembered her hands exploring him, caressing him while she'd kissed him, her tongue licking him, hot and wet. She drove him wild. He inhaled again and stretched, trying to get their lovemaking out of his mind.

It surprised him how often he thought of her. He'd always been able to keep whatever woman was in his life out of his thoughts. But Emily had a way of stirring memories too easily. Soon he was lost in erotic fantasies, wanting her badly.

Suppose she turned him down? Should he have another offer ready? He wasn't going to let her go. She had to have a price. He wanted Hub's inheritance…and the old man was slipping by the week.

Jake thought about his offer. He wondered if Emily would

sleep easily tonight. Her cheeks had been pink, her blue eyes stormy, but he'd been surprised how composed she'd remained.

She was getting to him in ways he didn't want. He wished he'd looked into her life more before they'd married. He'd had her background checked and she'd seemed perfect, a spotless record. She could run for public office without worry. But it had never occurred to him when he'd picked a woman who wasn't interested in his wealth, that she wouldn't be impressed by it, either.

He shook his head. He had to think clearly about his alternatives if she turned him down. He was not going to let Emily walk out on him. Not until he had Hub's inheritance.

# Four

Saturday morning Emily showered and dressed with care, pulling on a navy dress with a straight skirt that ended midcalf. It had a split up one side that revealed her legs when she walked. The neckline was high and the sleeves short. It was simple, and she liked how she looked in it. Her hair was combed and fell freely across her shoulders.

She'd spent a sleepless night, weighing her options and possibilities, trying to decide what would be best for her future and contemplating the consequences.

Promptly at half-past seven Jake called from the lobby and she told him to come up.

When she heard his faint knock, she swung open the door and her heart thudded.

Wearing one of his dark suits, he was at his most appealing...and formidable. Her mouth went dry and her pulse raced. She couldn't keep from glancing at his sensual, sculpted lips and thinking about his kisses. Trying to gather her wits, she inhaled. Jake looked confident and in control.

"You look gorgeous," he said.

"Thank you," she replied, walking away from him to put distance between them. She needed to stay on her toes, because she could feel a battle coming.

"How's the hotel? My friend's is just down the street if you care to move. I can get you a luxury suite."

"I'm comfortable where I am," she replied, wondering how long they would deal so courteously with each other. A moment of tense silence stretched between them.

"Have you decided? Do you accept my offer?" Jake asked.

"I've given it a lot of thought. I stayed up all night." She raised her chin. "You said you're always open to negotiation. You told me to learn to salvage what I can from a bad situation."

Amusement flashed in his eyes. "I did offer that advice."

"I hope I took it," she replied, trying to look calm. She didn't want to let him discover her palms were already damp. "You also advised me to always listen to the offer and weigh my options."

"I may have extended a bit more advice than I should have for my own good," he remarked dryly.

They were sparring, and at the moment she enjoyed it. But she also knew she was out of her league. Jake was an old hand at one-upmanship, and she felt as if she were tiptoeing through a verbal minefield.

"I've thought about everything, considered the possibilities and the future. I want the million you promised. I can't give that up," she said, and he smiled.

"I'm glad you faced reality. I hope you've calmed down," he said with satisfaction in his voice.

"I'm composed enough. I'll stay for the six months with a definite agreement that there will be no marital privileges. This will be a marriage on paper only."

"Agreed," he declared. "It sounds as if there's a condition coming. What are the terms? I have a feeling there's something you want besides the million dollars."

"You're astute as usual," she said, her pulse quickening as she braced for the storm she knew would follow. "I recall you saying to me, 'Do you think I'll miss it?' referring to the half a million you first offered me. No, you won't miss the money. It's pocket change to you. In your world, it's a paltry sum, so you're really not out anything on this so far, Jake." Her heart raced as he stared at her.

"I'm beginning to think I should stop offering you advice. A million dollars isn't exactly 'pocket change.' How much more do you want?" he persisted, watching her more intently now.

"I don't want more money," she replied, taking a deep breath. "Your world revolves around money. Mine doesn't. Mine is wound up with people and their needs."

"So?" he asked when she paused to take a breath. "What else do you want?"

"You. I want you to give four hours a week of your own time to coach some kids in football on Saturday afternoons."

"Hell! I'm not spending my valuable time with a bunch of kids," he snapped, his eyes flashing. "No way. Can't they get football coaching at school?"

"They could use some personal attention."

His dry laugh held no humor. "I'm not coaching any kids. Forget it, Emily! I don't want to deal with kids!" he exclaimed, losing his poise.

She'd stayed awake until four in the morning contemplating her future and weighing options. This was an opportunity to get what she wanted from him and at the same time to shake up his world and exact payment for his deception. Never again would she have such leverage with him. She didn't intend to back off now even if it cost her the million and the marriage, which was doomed, anyway.

"I don't imagine you do. But then, I don't want to move back in with you," she replied, trying to sound nonchalant and indifferent. In addition to getting back at him, she wanted to help the boys. And deep down, she knew Jake was still the person who was good to his family and good to friends. She suspected if she could reach him and make him really look at some of the world's problems, he'd do more to help solve them. Right now, she knew she was in for a battle.

"No," he said flatly. "That's an unreasonable demand. I use my time in far more productive ways."

"Productive to you. If you don't want to meet my terms, okay. We'll get our lawyers and dissolve our marriage," she said, her heart drumming. The air crackled with static as they clashed.

He stared at her and she stared back. She was glad she was across the room from him, because her heart was racing violently. Never in her life had she threatened anyone, but she was desperate and furious.

Silence stretched between them, taut sparks of friction flying. Silence and indecision was so unlike him, and her edginess grew. She knew he was trying to think of something—anything—to get what he wanted and avoid meeting her terms. He was a formidable adversary. That was the only way she saw him now—as an opponent.

She waited, uncertain whether to keep quiet or urge him to give her an answer. He stood as still as a statue, his expression impassive. She heard a car horn honk far in the distance, disrupting the silence that enveloped them like fog.

"Well?" she asked finally, certain he could hear her hammering heart.

"Dammit! I'll give you two million if you cut my coaching the kids," Jake bargained. "That's a damned good offer."

As elation bubbled in her, she tried to remain expressionless and composed. He wanted to bargain and he hadn't come up with anything that gave him an advantage.

She shook her head, hoping she continued sounding nonchalant. "My offer is firm—no coaching, no deal," she said.

"I won't do it, Emily. You'll lose the million."

"So be it," she answered, and prayed that she remained firm.

He glared at her and she knew he was thinking over options. "I won't be any good at working with a bunch of teens."

Again she had another surge of exhilaration. He hadn't turned her down. "You know a lot about football," she reminded him. "They're kids. You know more than they do. You'll be very skilled at it. You're successful at everything you do."

"I know nothing about teenage kids."

"Not so, Jake. You were one, once. You had friends. If nothing else, you'll muddle through somehow. Coach them or I walk out of your life," she threatened, praying she seemed confident. "It's only a handful of kids. You don't have a qualm about standing in front of a boardroom filled with executives who want to tear you to pieces. You thrive on competition. These kids will look up to you. I'll even go with you the first time and introduce you."

"Let me get this straight—if I give in to your demands,

you'll stay the six months in my house as my wife in name only. People will think we have a regular marriage, but you and I will know better. In turn, I pay you one million dollars and coach four kids. Is that correct?"

"Yes," she agreed.

Another silence stretched between them, and time passed while they stared at each other. Six months earlier, Jake's withering look would have terrified her into yielding to whatever he demanded. But all she had to do was think about his deception and she found the strength to face him unruffled. She didn't actually think she'd win, but she was curious to see just how money hungry Jake was. She had nothing to lose either way. She was leaving him sooner or later. How badly did he want the inheritance?

She stood as still as he, hoping nothing showed in her expression. He frowned, planting his hands on his hips. He raked a hand through his hair, and she could tell he was debating telling her to get out of his life.

"Is there any price you'd take to cut coaching the kids?" he asked finally. "That's something I can't do."

"Absolutely not," she replied.

"Dammit, Emily, you know you have me at a disadvantage. You know if we split, my inheritance goes out the window."

She hadn't known for certain, but to hear him say it made her pulse leap. He had to keep her as his wife or give up all hope of the billion-dollar inheritance. Yet what hope did he have if she lived in his house and he couldn't touch her? She wasn't going to give him a baby that way. She knew Jake figured he'd be able to seduce her, but she would deal with that when the time came. Right now, she was too angry with him to let him near her. She waited in silence.

"I don't want to pay all the money up front at once," he said finally. "We divide it. Otherwise, you could take the money and run."

"All right. I'll take half this week deposited into my account. I'll take care of it from there. Then you can pay the remaining half in three months."

He shook his head. "No. A third now, a third in three months and the final third after we've completed our bargain. That's fair and you know it."

She thought about it and nodded. A third of a million was still a lot of money, and she'd have it immediately. "Very well. I'll accept it in thirds."

He stood in silence, still weighing his options. She wondered how long it would take him to reach a decision. He raised his head and glared at her. "We have a deal. I'll coach the damned kids! But I promise you that they'll hate me and I'll hate them."

"Done!" she declared, her spirits soaring. She'd held out for a fantastic arrangement. "It'll do you good to get out again into the real world."

And she got one million dollars to use as she saw fit. She was no longer Jake's wife except on paper. He would work with the high-school boys and help them. She hoped she banked her elation enough that he had no idea how happy she was about her victory.

She would get through the six months, take the money and get a divorce. She studied her handsome husband and regrets tugged at her. They could have had so much…

She shook that thought out of her head. Jake was who he was—a man after money and power. To add to the mix, he had political ambitions that would drive him even harder.

His eyes narrowed and his expression changed as his gaze raked blatantly over her, as if she was naked. Her heart thudded and her mouth went dry. She wondered what was running through his mind. She'd have thought he'd be irate with her and want to leave. But the scalding look he gave her didn't say that he wanted to get away. It was filled with sizzling desire, transforming the clash between them into an entirely different tension.

She drew a deep breath and realized there was a chance Jake could seduce her if they were together often. Yet when she thought about his deception, her fury became an armor that would keep him at bay.

"Maybe I've never really seen you," he said. "I sure as hell didn't know this side of you." His voice was low, speculative, hot. She had expected his anger to continue, never anticipating this abrupt switch to a different kind of heat. "You've made a bargain with me, Emily," he said.

With deliberation he took off his coat and tossed it aside without ever taking his gaze from her.

Her pulse roared as he walked up to her and thrust his hands into her hair, tilting her head up abruptly. "What happened to the quiet cooperative secretary I married?" he asked, studying her with those piercing eyes.

"I'm not your secretary now, Jake," she answered, desire igniting beneath his scalding perusal. She wanted to tell him to take his hands off her. They had an agreement and he was already violating it, but the words were locked in her throat.

"You just bested me, Emily. Something few men have ever done and no woman has. We agreed not to have sex, but I can't recall any stipulations that I can never kiss you. This morning, you got your way and what you wanted. Now I'm going to take what *I* want," he said.

Her heart drummed as she gazed up at him, wanting him and angry with him at the same time, unable to shake either response to him. She shook her head. "No, you're not," she whispered, knowing she wasn't really putting up a fight at all.

"You want me to kiss you," he said. "It shows in your eyes. Tell me to leave you alone, Emily."

While he waited, his smoky eyes vanquishing her protest, his arm went around her waist. She wanted to shout at him to go away, but she couldn't. Her heart hammered and her lips tingled and her toes curled in anticipation. She ached for him and wondered whether she'd really won at all. She'd get what he promised, but he'd take what he wanted and she would give it to him willingly. No matter how furious with him she was, how much she didn't like or trust him, she couldn't refuse him.

His gaze went to her mouth and he leaned closer. She was certain he could see her pulse raging.

"No, Jake," she whispered.

"Everything in you is saying yes," he said with satisfaction lighting his eyes. His mouth covered hers, his tongue thrusting deep as if he could bend her will to his own.

Her exhilaration over winning evaporated. Enraged with him for his deception, she wanted to shout no, to stand up to him, yet she couldn't. Why was she letting him kiss her?

Thoughts spun away as his arm tightened and he leaned over her. She knew now she hadn't really won this major part of their battle.

He leaned down until she lost her balance and she clung to him while he kissed her. Trying to resist, she stood as still as a statue. But desire scalded her and she had to return his kiss, to stroke his tongue with hers, to kiss him deeply and run her hands over him.

Finally, he released her and looked down at her with a satisfied expression.

"Don't let it go to your head, Jake," she whispered. "You know you can kiss me and I can't resist, but I will say no to anything more. I'm not giving you a baby."

"We've made our bargain," he said, still leaning over her. His gaze was intense, hot with desire. He swung her up and kissed her hard again, wrapping his arms around her.

His arousal thrust against her and she burst into flame, her breath ragged. She hoped she could live up to her words. She wouldn't let Jake get her pregnant. She knew he intended to seduce her, get her pregnant and inherit the money, but she wasn't having his baby.

She kissed him back for a moment, returning it passionately. A part of her wanted to excite him, frustrate him as much as he frustrated her. She thrust her tongue deep in his mouth, stroking and teasing, nipping his lower lip lightly, rubbing against his hard erection.

She felt him inhale, heard a groan deep in his throat. He released her and both of them gasped for breath as they studied each other.

Contradicting the storm in his gray eyes, he placed his palm gently against her cheek. "You're beautiful, Em. You absolutely take my breath away."

"How many women have you said that to?" she asked. His jaw hardened and his eyes turned cold.

"Want me to take you to breakfast?" he asked, instead of replying to her question. "After all, you have to eat and it'll save you money for your charities. We'll be in public so there'll be no more kisses. Get your purse and come with me. We don't even have to talk." Without waiting for her answer, he turned away to pick up his jacket and pull it on.

In consternation, she started to refuse. But she knew that everything Jake had just said was the truth, so why not let him buy her breakfast? Maybe she could torment him a little more.

In silence she picked up her purse, but paused when she noticed Jake had pulled out his cell phone. "I'll call my accountant. He'll have your bank account number and can transfer the first payment to you this morning," Jake said.

"Thank you," she said. She made a mental note to open another account that Jake and his staff knew nothing about and move the money. She intended to spend a lot of it as soon as possible, having decided already what she wanted to do and which projects were the most vital. A chunk of the money would go to her father's church. Her relationship with Jake was so volatile, she wanted to grab the money and run, get it spent so Jake couldn't take it back.

Barely able to hear his low voice, she listened as he gave the information to his head accountant. Then Jake clicked shut his phone. "It's done. Now you've got a lot of money to spread goodwill over Dallas."

"Thank you," she said. "So are we ready?"

He waved his hand toward the door and opened it for her. She swept out ahead of him and he fell into step beside her as they moved to the elevator.

They walked to the car in silence. She was aware of his height, his shoulder occasionally brushing hers. At the car, he reached around her to open the door for her and she caught the scent of his aftershave.

As she slid into the car, she glanced up to see him looking

down at her legs. Her skirt had fallen open at the slit, revealing her long legs.

"Thanks," she said perfunctorily, looking forward and trying to ignore him—which was totally impossible. He walked
around the front of the sports car, taking his usual long strides
that conveyed self-assurance in every step.

At the restaurant, as they followed the maître d' to a linen-
covered table, skylights let sunshine spill into the dining room.
Emily was aware of women turning to look at Jake. Women
gravitated to him like iron filings to a magnet. A lot of them
wouldn't have cared what Jake's motives were for marriage.
They'd be deliriously happy with all he could give them. Was
she being unreasonable? She didn't think so. As far as she was
concerned, deception was an unforgivable breach of trust.

Jake held her chair, his fingers barely brushing her, so
slight on her back and arm that it could have been accidental.
But she suspected Jake did very little unintentionally.

He sat across from her and once again, she could see faint
amusement in his eyes. He was so damn certain of himself.
He knew that he was handsome and sexy and that she couldn't
resist his kisses.

A waitress placed menus in front of them. Emily opened
hers and tried to ignore the sparks that danced between them
every time she glanced at Jake.

She ordered a huge breakfast, figuring she'd skip lunch and
eat on his dime.

With a wink for Jake, the waitress took their menus. Emily
looked into Jake's eyes. "You do impress women everywhere
you go," she said.

"There's one I don't impress enough," he replied. "So if
I'd refused to coach, would you really have walked? Admit

it, Em. We have a deal now and the money is being moved. Would you have walked out on the million?"

"Yes, I would," she said. "It doesn't seem real to me at this point, anyway."

"After over a year of being married to me, I don't see how it can't seem real. Of all the women in the world, I picked the one who isn't interested in wealth or luxury."

"As I recall," she said, smiling at him, "you said that's what you were searching for."

"Not to this extent. It never occurred to me anyone would react to money the way you do." He touched her cheek. "I don't usually miss the mark as I have with you. Maybe I'm losing my touch."

"Jake, as the old saying goes, you can't win 'em all. You always expect to win, that much I know about you. But nobody gets what they want all the time."

"True," he said, smiling at her with a flash of white teeth in a warm grin that was an invitation to relax her guard. She wondered how many times he'd coaxed what he wanted out of women with that irresistible smile. And she was as vulnerable to it as any of them.

"Are you free late this afternoon?" she asked sweetly, smiling at him in turn, sure she couldn't do to him what he could to her.

Pleasure flashed in his eyes. "Sure, I'm free," he said, reaching over to take her hand in his and lightly rub his thumb across her knuckles. Tingles spun from his touch, fanning an ever smoldering blaze. "And, for you, if I weren't, I'd get free. What did you have in mind?"

"I'll call this morning and see if I can catch the boys. You can start coaching late this afternoon," she said. Jake would hate to start today—all the more reason to make him do so, as far as she was concerned.

Instantly, his eyes turned glacial. He dropped her hand and sat back. "Dammit, Emily, this coaching thing is going to be disastrous. Football is history in my life. And I'm not a teacher."

"You're a smart man, Jake, and these are good kids. You'll manage." She paused while the waitress appeared with orange juice and cups of steaming coffee.

She fussed over Jake and then left them. "I don't think our waitress has noticed my wedding ring." Emily laughed. "Let me tell you about the boys. Orlando Crane and Anthony Day are American. The other two haven't been in this country long. English is their second language."

"Dammit, Emily! I can't talk to them?"

"Oh, please!" she exclaimed, exasperated. "You travel and do business all over the world," she said, her anger flaring at his stubborn refusal to cooperate. "How many languages do you speak?" Jake clamped his mouth shut and the glacial look returned to his expression. Undaunted, she continued, "Enzo Oquendo is Costa Rican and Tanek Kozlik is from Germany, but that wasn't where he was born."

Suddenly Jake sat back and relaxed, a crooked smile tugging up one corner of his mouth. "I can't believe you've managed this." He leaned forward over the table and his voice dropped. "I want you, Em. I want to make love to you and to get through that iron wall of anger you've thrown up between us."

Her pulse drummed and her nipples became taut as his gaze drifted languidly over her. She wound her fingers together in her lap and hoped she could maintain the iron wall of anger he referred to. "This is one time you won't be getting your way. You brought it on yourself," she whispered, leaning toward him; she looked into his eyes and saw the tiny flecks of green near his pupils. "You're not going to make love to me."

"We'll see, Em," he whispered, touching her throat.

"You want me to need you and beg for your loving, to get wild with you so you can flaunt that male dominance of yours. Not this time," she said, shaking her head and hoping with all her heart she could live up to her words. Looking into his thickly lashed eyes, she was thankful they were out in public because she was melting right now. Her knees were weak, her insides jelly and she was hot, wanting him and trying to bank the hot images his words called to mind.

"Perhaps. Challenges are always interesting," he said. Again she received one of those come-hither, crooked smiles that was as seductive as a caress. He drew his fingers along her throat lightly, and she knew her racing pulse would give him satisfaction.

To her relief their waitress appeared with their breakfasts, placing a golden omelet in front of her, along with crisp strips of bacon, flaky biscuits and a bowl of fruit with ripe red strawberries, blueberries and chunks of green melon. She still had no appetite, but knew she should eat. She hadn't eaten a thing yesterday.

"When I get back to the hotel, the first thing I'll do is try to make arrangements for this afternoon. I'll go with you to introduce you to the boys and I'll bring refreshments."

Jake looked amused. "If I have to do this, I'll get the damn refreshments so you don't have to lug around a cooler. What do they want—cold beer?"

"Don't you dare take beer to those boys!" she snapped. "Take some soda and get them a pizza and sandwiches. Get them candy bars and cookies, too. They're always hungry."

"So am I," Jake said in a silky voice, letting his gaze roam over her. She knew he wasn't thinking about food.

"Jake, pay attention," she said.

"I am," he answered with great innocence. "I like to flirt with you, Em."

"That time has passed," she replied firmly.

He reached over to take her wrist and place his thumb on her pulse. His lips curved in satisfaction. "I don't think so. Your pulse gives me a different answer."

Glaring at him, she ate in silence, wanting to return to the hotel and get on with her day. Jake was touching, flirting and trying to beguile her. Everything he was doing was having an effect on her. What woman could resist him when he turned on the charm?

"So tell me about these kids. Why are they important to you?" he asked.

"I know Orlando and Anthony through Dad's church. They both tutor kids on Wednesday nights. Anthony comes from a broken home. His dad is not around, he has lots of brothers and sisters and he ran away a few months ago. I don't think his mother cared. To keep him off the street, Orlando took him home. There's no dad in that household, either, but his mother and grandmother are good people and Orlando is bright." She wondered if Jake was even listening. She doubted she'd stirred one shred of sympathy. "The other two families have come here to try to better their lives."

"All very touching, Em. You're a bleeding heart, but I suppose that's the way you were raised. When you're dad's a minister, that's probably all you know."

"You're hopeless! I expect you to live up to your part of the bargain."

"Sure. And you live up to yours."

She nodded and put down her fork. She'd eaten all she could, but she sipped a little more hot coffee and drank her orange juice.

"We could spend the day together until I have to meet the boys. I can cancel anything I have if you'll get free."

She shook her head. "No, thanks. I have things to do—without you, Jake. Be thankful for what you've got from me and let it go at that."

"I'm intrigued. You're a different person than the one I thought I married. I want to get to know you."

"You should have thought of that a long time ago. And you should have realized that I prefer honesty over deception."

"I'll remember that."

She finished her coffee and waved the waitress away when she returned for refills and to flirt with Jake.

Jake took Emily back to the hotel, driving through sunny streets that were already growing warm. He stopped beyond the front door so the doorman wouldn't bother them.

"Thanks for breakfast," she said, holding the door handle. "I'll call you as soon as I make arrangements for this afternoon."

Jake gazed at her speculatively, and she wondered what he was thinking. He merely nodded. "You know how to get me. Want me to help you move home? I can get someone to take your things and pick you up."

"I'll manage, thank you," she answered sweetly.

He stepped out so swiftly, she didn't even have her door open. He came around the car to hold the door for her and she climbed out, looking up at him. He stood a fraction too close and her pulse jumped. "Thanks for breakfast," she repeated, not even realizing what she was saying to him.

"Sure," Jake replied. And as she walked away, she could feel him watching her. She hadn't heard him close her door yet and knew he must be still standing there. Her back tingled and she moved slightly faster, wanting to get into the hotel.

The minute she was in her room, she tossed aside her purse and let out her breath. The morning had taken a toll. She berated herself for succumbing to his charm, for kissing him back, for responding in every way to him.

When she thought about what she'd wrung out of him, she threw up her hands. She'd won a victory of sorts over Jake and she might as well enjoy it while it lasted. She'd gotten a bit of revenge for his deception, making him pay for it with the million dollars to her and an even bigger concession— coaching the kids. "I won, Jake!" she exclaimed aloud, spinning around in celebration. "I won! Serves you right for what you did!"

She walked out to the balcony to look below, but Jake's car was nowhere in sight.

# Five

Jake watched Emily hurry into the hotel. The slight sway of her hips was sexy, and when he looked at the thick curtain of brown hair that swung with each step, he thought about his fingers wrapped in its softness. He wanted her. She could arouse him with a look or a sentence or a touch—too many ways. He suspected she had no idea of the effect she had on him.

He'd never really seen her before. He thought he had her all figured out—quiet and sweet and intelligent, very efficient in an office. But he'd ditched that image. That wasn't the woman who'd laid down terms for him to meet this morning and wrung an agreement out of him. As she disappeared into the hotel he slammed the car door shut, got behind the wheel and drove away.

Damned if she hadn't bested him this morning! He shook his head and had to laugh at himself. He'd broken one of his hard-and-fast rules for negotiation—never underestimate your opponent. He'd underestimated Emily by a country mile. All because of stupid carelessness on his part. He really should have tossed the letter.

He remembered Emily in his arms, her blue eyes widening, her pulse racing. She couldn't say no to his kisses. Jake shifted uncomfortably. He got hot and hard just thinking about those kisses. She had always turned him on easily, but now she did it more easily than ever.

He vowed he'd have her in his bed within the month. Hopefully, within the week. If she stayed in his house, they'd be together and he was going to do his damnedest to seduce her.

She was sexy, passionate and more responsive than any other woman he'd known. She set him on fire. He'd been angry, wanting to subdue her to his will. Instead, he'd stirred her passion and she'd melted him with her kisses.

Except for their difficulty getting pregnant, this had been a good match. Until she found the letter. Damn, why hadn't he destroyed it at once? If she hadn't found it…

He had to stop speculating! She'd found it and there was nothing he could do to change that. But a baby would solve everything. Trying to get Em pregnant had been the best part of his life.

The thought itself astounded him. Making love to her had become important to him.

What would happen if she wanted to walk out on him when their six months were up? He was certain he could prevent it just as he had now. Everyone had a price and he knew Emily's. Although she *had* surprised him. He vowed he would not underestimate her a second time.

Driving home, he thought about the coming week, the

business calls he had to make. But within minutes, his thoughts slid back to Emily.

The kitten had claws, he'd found out. She'd driven a difficult bargain and one he didn't care to honor. He could give up the money, but damned if he wanted to waste his time each week with a handful of high-school kids.

He shook his head ruefully. Most women he knew would have dropped it instantly at the promise of diamonds or a fancy car or a month at a luxury spa. Not practical Emily.

Visions of her naked in his arms taunted him, and he inhaled deeply, trying to shift his mind elsewhere.

He swept through the tall, electronic wrought-iron gates to his thirty-acre property. Irritated over the prospects for the afternoon, Jake sped up the drive to his sprawling 22,000-square-foot three-story hilltop mansion overlooking a twenty-five-acre lake. The stately Corinthian columns spread along the lengthy verandas and the upper balconies. Jake drove toward the nine-car garage, parked in the circular drive in front of it and strode in through an entry hall that led into a kitchen where his chef greeted him.

"Welcome back, Mr. Thorne," the gray-haired man said, lifting a covered pan out of an oven.

"Morning, Charley. Smells enticing in here. It's been too long since I've eaten one of your delicious meals," he said. "Your cooking is one of the good things about coming home."

"Thank you, sir." Charley took the lid off a pan, allowing steam and the inviting smells of a succulent roast to escape into the room.

If he stopped to think about it, Jake was ever grateful he'd been able to hire Charley away from the elegant Chicago restaurant where he'd been chef. Unless he was needed for a special event, Charley worked four days a week, leaving enough food prepared for the other three.

"I'm already hungry in spite of just eating breakfast," Jake said, crossing the large kitchen and walking through the breakfast room with its oak fireplace and polished oak floors. Hopefully, he could talk Emily into eating dinner with him. As he passed through the room, he greeted Olive, the head of his household cleaning staff,

Strolling down a wide hallway to the large open area of his main living room, he looked up at the soaring twenty-foot ceiling with the large crystal chandeliers he'd bought in France. His gaze passed over the pale-yellow walls, the curving double staircase and row of French doors that opened to the terrace. He remembered the first time he'd brought Emily home with him, She'd stopped in the foyer beside his marble fountain and stood staring at the room, taking in antiques, elegant furniture, marble floors.

"Jake, you live in a palace!" she'd exclaimed.

"I like beautiful things, my houses, my gardens, my pools, my cars, my wife," he said, turning to take her arm. "I'll show you around in a while, but first I have other plans," he said in a husky voice. He'd given all his staff a week off. Meals had been prepared for them, and he hadn't wanted anyone around. "Come here, Em," he said.

Her wide-eyed look changed instantly as she shifted her attention to him. "Jake," she whispered, sliding her arm around his neck as he pulled her to him.

But as he peeled away her silk blouse, she leaned away and glanced around. "Jake, this house is so open. With all the glass, we don't have privacy." She continued to look around. "You must have staff to keep this…"

"I have a large staff that I'll introduce you to next week. In the meantime, we have all the privacy we could possibly want. My staff is gone and there's a high wall surrounding the house equipped with electronic surveillance equipment. And another privacy wall surrounds the grounds with even more surveillance. No one will disturb us. This property is secure and private."

"I knew you were wealthy," she said, studying him, "but I never imagined all this."

He shrugged. "So is that a plus or minus in your eyes?"

She inhaled and glanced around. "Neither. Something I'll just have to get used to. My lifestyle has been a world apart from yours."

"No longer," he'd said, leaning down to trail kisses along her throat and cup her breast in his hand, hearing her gasp of pleasure and knowing he'd taken her mind off his house and wealth.

Jake shook himself out of memories. He was aroused, but determined to wipe her out of his thoughts.

He took the stairs two at a time to the second floor and strode along the wide hallway that overlooked the living area on one side and the gardens on the other. At the end of the hallway, he turned toward the master bedroom suite with its adjoining exercise room, nearby office and morning kitchen.

He strode across the sitting room of the master suite to his closet, where he changed into shorts and a T-shirt and went to exercise, determined to get Emily out of his thoughts for at least an hour.

He worked out fiercely, then headed down to the pool to swim laps. He tried to avoid glancing toward the chaise longue where he'd made passionate love to Emily.

After a shower, Jake dressed in navy slacks and a navy knit shirt. He spent the next hours in calls and at his computer, finally stopping in the afternoon. When the phone rang, he answered to hear Emily's voice.

"Jake, I've talked to the boys and they'll be at the practice field at four o'clock. I'll have my bags loaded in my car here at the hotel and I'll just meet you there. Let me give you the address. Do you have a pen?"

"Go ahead," he said and scribbled the address, frowning when he realized where he'd be going. "That's a tough part of town."

"Scared, Jake?" she asked.

Anger flashed, but at the same time, he grinned because she was taunting him. "Not for me, but I'm not enthused about you driving there alone."

"I'm fine, Jake. I visit the high school for projects I'm involved in all the time."

"Dammit, you shouldn't be doing that."

"I'll meet you. You'll still get the refreshments?"

"Yes, I will. Dammit, Emily—"

"Stop swearing. After you meet them, you'll like them."

"Oh, sure," he said dryly. "Eat dinner here with me tonight."

"Fine," she answered casually. "See you at four." The line went dead and he swore again. He did not want to deal with a bunch of kids. He shook his head. He'd gotten himself into this one, but he was going to make Emily pay in the most pleasurable way possible.

That afternoon, Emily headed over to the high school. Jittery and on edge, she wasn't sure if Jake would even show up. She couldn't imagine Jake would really find any task daunting and suspected he simply saw this as a colossal waste of his time and energy.

The school was in one of the older areas of town. Yards were filled with cars, some on concrete blocks. A few houses were boarded up. Some needed a coat of paint. The high school itself was an aging brick building that stood in stark contrast to the plush surroundings she inhabited now.

Jake was parked by the practice field. His Jaguar stood out with the sparkle of a diamond dropped in ashes. She slowed and stopped behind Jake's car, her pulse racing.

Across the field, she saw the boys lounging on dilapidated bleachers that had collapsed at one end.

Jake stepped out into bright sunshine in jeans and a T-shirt, his hands on his hips as he waited. When she emerged from her car, his gaze slowly drifted over her blue T-shirt and jeans. Tingles zinged to her toes beneath his obviously appreciative gaze as she approached him. Each time she saw him, she reacted to him and couldn't keep from thinking how handsome he was.

"I can think of a far better way to spend the next hour," he drawled, and her pulse sped another notch. There was no mistaking the innuendo in his husky voice or the look in his eye.

"I appreciate this, Jake. And you'll never know how much it'll mean to those kids."

"I doubt that. You probably coerced them into this as much as you did me," he said, hitting closer to the truth than she wanted to admit. The boys had been less than enthusiastic, but she wanted Jake to get to know them, to spend time with people who grew up the way he did. She thought he'd lost his perspective and lived a life that shielded him from people he could help.

"You'll charm them. Trust me, you'll win them over," she said, linking her arm through his and tugging lightly to lead him toward the boys.

Even though he walked beside her, she could still feel the tension and clash of wills between them and knew Jake was hating every moment. "You have facets to you, Emily, that I never realized before. Today has been an eye-opener."

"I think it's best I don't ask whether you like what you've discovered," she said lightly. But she suspected Jake was seething over this whole arrangement. She knew she was taunting a tiger.

"These guys are high school?" Jake asked under his breath as they approached the four boys who sat sprawled on the bleachers and made no move to get up.

"Remember, they're football players, so they're big. Enzo and Tanek are juniors, and Orlando and Anthony are seniors this year."

"Emily, I was a damn field-goal kicker, not a lineman. Those bruisers are linemen."

"But you're not afraid to work with them. It wouldn't matter if they were half again as big. You'll manage." Without waiting for his answer, she continued, "You can reach them. Don't act like this is insurmountable. They're like you were at one time."

"Not exactly," he said, eyeing the group as they drew closer. "Dammit!"

She could hear the anger in Jake's voice. She'd make introductions and leave him on his own—she had no doubt that once she was out of the picture, Jake would take charge. It would take time to reach the kids, but eventually he'd work with them to everyone's benefit. Her heart fluttered and her palms were damp. What if Jake walked out? No, they'd made a deal and she expected him to stick by it.

They halted near the bleachers. "Hi!" Emily said, greeting

the guys with a smile. She received smiles and warm greetings in return.

She still had her arm through Jake's. "I want all of you to meet my husband. I've told you about his football years. This is Jake Thorne." She looked at Orlando, the leader of the boys. The first day she'd met them, he'd taken charge. He was a natural leader. While he and Jake might clash, this was the one whose lead the others would follow. He was also the one she was most interested in Jake getting to know.

"Orlando Crane, this is Jake." She stared at Orlando, who was seated with his legs apart, elbows on knees, his thick blond hair a curly mat on his thick neck. His sleeveless T-shirt revealed powerful, sculpted biceps. He held a football in his hands. His blue eyes shifted to Emily as he unfolded, standing and tucking the football under his arm. To her relief Jake offered his hand and Orlando shook it, enveloping Jake's hand in his. They were the same height, but she suspected Orlando might have thirty pounds on Jake.

Jake's eyes conveyed his fury, and she wondered if he would honor his bargain. She knew he wasn't a quitter. She turned to a boy stretched on his side with his slender blond head propped on his hand. "Tanek Kozlik," she said, then paused. He glanced at Orlando and then stood, jumping down off the bleachers and coming forward to shake Jake's hand. By that time, the other two guys came to their feet and approached Jake.

Tanek was two inches taller than Jake, she guessed, and perhaps fifty pounds heavier. "Nice wheels," he said to Jake in heavily accented English.

"Anthony Day, meet Jake Thorne," she said to a young man with powerful muscles, ebony skin and a compact body. He was inches shorter than the other guys, under six feet she was certain, but he played football and was friends with the others. Anthony gave Jake a friendly grin and she was grateful that he seemed receptive. Although, she knew that might not be the case when she was no longer around.

She turned to the last guy, a black-haired boy from Costa Rica, Enzo Oquendo, who shook hands in silence with Jake.

"I'll get out of the way," she said, "but before I go, I know Jake brought some drinks and a few snacks. Tanek, if you and Enzo would come with me, I'll get everything out of Jake's car and you can bring them back here," she said, deliberately leaving Jake to get to know Orlando and Anthony better before they started. One last look at Jake's smoldering gray eyes caused her to stand on tiptoe and brush Jake's cheek with a kiss.

"See you later," she said lightly. "Orlando, Anthony, I'll see you next week." She knew she'd see them when they tutored the elementary-school kids.

Together with the two boys, she crossed the field and opened the trunk of Jake's car, getting out a cooler and insulated containers that held the pizzas. That should help smooth over the afternoon. The two thanked her and told her goodbye, friendly as ever. She hoped Jake had as easy a time with them.

As she climbed behind the wheel, she saw Jake talking to Orlando and Anthony, and she said a small prayer that all would go well.

On the long winding drive to Jake's palatial Dallas home, her anger with him returned. Jake had deceived her for money he didn't need. The three-story mansion was stunning. The first level had a billiards room, game room, exercise room and theater. There was both a banquet room and a smaller dining room, and a paneled bar and wine cellar. Growing familiar with the mansion had included getting to know his staff. It had taken her weeks to meet and get to know everyone, particularly those she seldom saw. She was constantly reminded that he didn't need to inherit more money.

She had spent the morning on her cell phone, consulting an accountant, talking to her father and others who ran the organizations where she intended her money to go. Monday, she wanted to start getting it moved so it would be out of Jake's reach.

She thought about going to visit her parents, getting away from Jake. But Saturday night was a busy time for her father, so she decided she'd get through tonight at the mansion and see her parents tomorrow night.

She showered and changed into a red silk lounging outfit, deciding to skip dinner and avoid Jake tonight as much as possible. She had one of the staff carry her suitcases to a guest bedroom at the far end of the hall from the master bedroom. She'd ruled out the third-floor bedrooms as too inconvenient and decided the opposite wing on the second floor would be far enough from Jake.

She was still gathering clothes, packing more to move to her own bedroom when she heard Jake coming down the hall. She glanced at her watch and saw that Jake was an hour earlier than she'd expected. He charged into the room and she was jolted by his stormy gaze.

"Jake! What happened?"

"Dammit, Emily! If I didn't work out, they would've killed me," Jake said, crossing the room in long angry strides. He had a dark smudge of dirt on his cheek, his sleeve was torn and his T-shirt had grass stains. Otherwise, he looked fine and far from injured.

He held her shoulders, leaning close with his eyes blazing. "You knew they'd do that! They didn't want this any more than I did!"

"Maybe they didn't," she said, stiffening and glaring back at him. "But you'll win them over. I know you can if you want to. If money was at stake here, you'd go after it like a starving man after food."

"I don't want to do this!"

"You have a choice," she came back at him. In spite of the anger flying between them, Jake's wavy black hair fell over his forehead and he looked as desirable as ever. "Take your hands off me, Jake!" she snapped, her pulse drumming. "You'll survive."

His gaze lowered and he thrust her away from him, looking at her slowly from her head to her toes. His hot gaze was as tangible as a caress and she could see the change in his expression. A muscle worked in his jaw, but now desire blazed where anger had been. He looked into her eyes and she lost her breath.

"Dammit, Emily," he said, his voice thick and husky now. Her insides tangled and knotted as her lips parted.

"Are you hurt?" she asked.

He shook his head. "No thanks to you," he said, grinding the words out as he wound his hand in her hair and tilted her head back. "They would have beaten me to a pulp if they could have."

"I can't believe that! They're nice polite boys—"

"The hell they are!" He leaned down to kiss her throat. "The deal's off," he said.

"If the deal's off, I don't stay, Jake," she announced, closing her eyes and swaying closer. "You'll win them over," she said, forgetting football, kids and her bargain with Jake. "Stop kissing me," she said in a whisper with the force of melted butter.

"You don't mean that," he said. "Dammit, I'm not coaching them," he repeated, and covered her mouth before she could reply.

Why was she in his arms? Why was she kissing him in return? She'd spent the past two days furious with him. So why couldn't she resist him the second his mouth touched hers? She'd kissed plenty of men she could resist. Why couldn't she withstand Jake? As his arms enveloped her and he kissed her passionately, she stopped worrying about it.

How long they kissed, she didn't know. Nor did she notice Jake unbuttoning her blouse. But when he shoved aside the silk and her bra to caress her breasts, she gasped with pleasure. It was just the jolt she needed to realize that if she didn't stop him right away, she wouldn't at all.

She caught his wrist. "Jake, wait," she said, pushing against his chest and then pushing again, harder this time. When he released her slightly, she gulped for air and pulled her blouse together. Desire darkened his expression, making it more difficult for her to tell him no.

"We have an arrangement," she said, wriggling out of his embrace and walking away from him as she swiftly buttoned her blouse.

She turned to find him aroused and looking at her with such hunger she wondered if he would try to kiss her again in spite of her protests.

"I'll cook steaks for us," he said. And then he left the room, slamming the door behind him.

She was startled at his abrupt departure. "I don't want to eat dinner with you," she said to the closed door. With shaking hands, she changed to jeans and a T-shirt as swiftly as she could. Jamming her feet into loafers, she snatched up her purse and left, hurrying downstairs to her car to drive away. She knew she should've just told Jake she wouldn't eat with him, instead of running the minute his back was turned. But she was tired of Jake getting his way about everything.

Glancing in the rearview mirror, she wondered how much she would anger Jake by standing him up for dinner. She was certain that had probably never happened before in his life, but she didn't care. She didn't want to be in his arms tonight, to battle the charm that could mesmerize and seduce her. He was probably in the outdoor kitchen now, an elegant area adjoining the back of the house that had the most elaborate barbecue she'd ever seen. Jake had radiant-heat flagstones under the veranda flagstones for when the weather turned chilly. Cool air piped out on hot nights for summer parties. He didn't need Hubert Braden's inheritance in the least.

She drove aimlessly for a time and then stopped to call her folks. To her delight, her father was already prepared for Sunday morning and they weren't busy. Plus her sister and one of her brothers were there with two nieces and a nephew.

Eagerly, she climbed back in her car and headed for her parents' house, relieved to know she would have a night away from Jake and all his manipulation.

Jake stripped down and stepped into a shower, wishing he had Emily with him, hoping the hot water would take away his aches and save him even more pain and stiffness tomorrow. He'd meant what he'd said to her. If he didn't work out for at least an hour every day, he wasn't sure he would have been able to crawl off that field.

Clamping his jaw closed, he stood, relishing the hot spray over his throbbing muscles while he thought about dinner with Emily. Dressed in the red silk, she had been irresistible, a tempting flame. His fury and frustration had rolled over into white-hot desire. And she had kissed him back. Her anger and her reluctance, her coldness, were shallow. He could easily get past them—he already had twice today.

His pulse sped up in anticipation of dinner with her. He dressed in charcoal slacks and a black knit shirt and strode out of his closet, glancing at his king-size bed, seeing Emily sprawled naked on it. He told himself to go slow tonight, flirt, kiss her, build the fires in her. She was too passionate to keep saying no to him.

He whistled as he combed his hair. Eagerness had him hurrying down the hall to her room. The door stood open, and he decided she must have already gone downstairs.

After searching the kitchen, the living rooms and the terraces, he looked to see if her car was in the driveway.

She was gone! Annoyed, but loath to spend the evening at the house by himself, he thought about where she could have gone. She probably went to visit her family. If she wasn't there, he'd give up looking. But going to her family's house might mean he could at least spend the evening with her. Her friendly family wouldn't turn him away.

Her father answered his phone call and within a minute Jake had an invitation to join them.

Then Emily said hello and Jake could feel the chill in her tone.

"Your dad is his usual jovial self and invited me out for the evening," Jake said.

"Jake, I intended to spend the night here by myself."

"I miss you and told your dad I'd come out."

"Did you hear what I just told you," she repeated, speaking softly and he knew that she not only didn't want him to visit, she didn't want her family to overhear her part of their conversation.

"Maybe you'll change your mind, Emily," Jake replied lightly.

"Don't. I need to go now," she said and broke the connection.

She obviously hadn't told her family that she and Jake were having trouble. Shortly, he was back in his car, leaving a sumptuous-looking steak in the fridge as he sped away toward her parents' house.

By now he knew Emily's background was modest, but in many ways more comfortable than his had been. They'd moved several times when she was growing up as her father had been assigned to different churches, but now her folks lived in Dallas in a home her father owned. Her brother, Will, and his family lived nearby, her sister, Beth, in the suburbs and the other brothers in Austin and Houston.

Jake liked her family. It was the sort he'd often dreamed about as a kid. Everyone loved each other and got along. Her three brothers had been slightly reserved at first, but it hadn't lasted. Beth's auburn-haired husband, Decklin, had been friendly from the start.

Jake thought about his own sister, Nina, married two years now with no children and practicing law in Florida. His mother, who lived two miles from Nina, wasn't the grandmotherly type. He didn't think she was waiting anxiously for either of them to give her a grandchild.

Jake drove through the tree-lined neighborhood of two-story houses in brick and stone, finally turning at a small house where a porch light was on and cars were in the drive.

He parked, crossed the porch and strode to the front door

to ring the bell. The door swung open and three kids spilled out. His pulse jumped at the sight of Emily in jeans, a navy knit shirt, her hair caught in a barrette behind her head.

Shooing the kids in and stepping outside, she pulled the door closed behind her. "Why are you here, Jake? This is the one place where I can resist your touch, so there's not much reason for you to have come."

"I wanted to spend the evening with you. I like your family, too," he said, looking down into her wide blue eyes. He wondered whether she was going to send him on his way right now. He wanted to touch her, but he kept his hands to himself. "I missed you."

# Six

Emily stared at Jake in consternation even while her heart skipped beats at the sight of him. She didn't want her parents to know yet about the rift between Jake and her or the impending end of their marriage. They would worry for the next six months, and she didn't want that. When the time came to leave Jake, it would be over and done quickly, and they would find out. Earlier tonight, she'd confided in her sister about her failing marriage, but Beth would keep the news to herself.

In the meantime, Emily knew she had to be pleasant to Jake and let him in the house, even though she would like to close the door in his handsome face.

"I wanted to be with you, Emily," he repeated when she stared at him in silence.

"Please, Jake—when you're absorbed in your own problems and earning more money, you don't mind being away from me." She glanced over her shoulder and then back. "You're here, so come in for a while."

Inside, she occasionally thought about the difference between Jake's lavish homes and her parents' simpler one. She inhaled the smells of hot bread and the tangy aroma of beef and barbeque that pervaded the entire house. "We've eaten already," she said. She was interrupted by her mother who appeared with a smile, coming forward to give Jake a hug. Emily watched while her family poured out to greet him.

They had always teased her because she was the reserved one in the family. Her ruddy-cheeked father had a smile for everyone, and her mother was full of hugs for friends and family. Beth took after her mother, and her brothers were like her father. Emily was the only one who stood back and observed the world quietly. She had been teased about it all her life, but that was her nature and she was comfortable with it.

She watched her family greet Jake. Her five-year-old niece, four-year-old niece and three-year-old nephew said a quick hello and ran off to play. She'd noticed that children paid little attention to Jake and he didn't give heed to them. From the start she had wondered what kind of father he'd make, but now she knew that his anticipation of fatherhood had been backed by a goal that had nothing to do with his love for children.

Her father and brother, Will, whisked Jake off to the family room while she returned to the kitchen to help clean up.

Later the family settled in the living room to play a game of cards. She held her sleepy nephew, Sean, on her lap and wondered whether Jake was letting others win. Jake was the most competitive person she'd ever known and she was certain he was holding himself in check. As usual, he'd turned on the charm and her family was entranced.

By eleven her father announced that he had to turn in. Emily glanced at Jake. "I'll see you to the door, Jake," she said, standing.

"Nonsense!" her mother exclaimed. "Emily! We're not sending Jake home at this hour. Jake, you'll stay, won't you? Both of you, stay and join us for Sunday dinner after church tomorrow."

"Mom, Jake and I aren't dressed for church," Emily cut in quickly before Jake could answer.

"Don't be ridiculous," her mother said. "You look nice. It's still warm out and some people dress casually. Besides, I can loan you a skirt and blouse if you like. Both of you are fine."

"Thanks, Bea," Jake said easily. "I'd love to join the family and hear Al's sermon."

"Then it's settled," her mother said, smiling and gathering up cards while Beth took Sean from Emily's arms.

"As soon as I put him down, let's have hot chocolate before Decklin and I have to hit the road," Beth suggested. Frustrated and angry with Jake for intruding, Emily was willing to do anything to put off the moment she had to go to her small bedroom where they usually shared a double bed. Soon her sister would leave and her brother, too, would gather up his brood and go. If she and Jake didn't share the same bedroom tonight and her mother or her father discovered it, there would be endless questions she didn't want to answer. Better at this point to deal with Jake than her parents. She looked at him, meeting his gaze and wondering what he was thinking. He arched one dark eyebrow and she looked away.

It was one in the morning when they finally went to the small bedroom she'd shared with her sister years earlier. She wondered what Jake really thought about her family. He was always charming and polite. He'd given them some lavish gifts, including a new car for her parents, and she had to admit that Jake had poured money into her father's mission projects. Yet now she felt everything Jake had done had an ulterior motive, each bringing him one step closer to a huge inheritance.

The small bedroom seemed claustrophobic, and Jake dominated it as he closed the door and turned to study her. "The house was empty without you."

"Oh, please, Jake," she said.

She looked at the bed. It seemed postage-stamp size now. In the past, Jake had filled it with his feet hanging off. "I'm not getting into that bed with you," she said softly.

He shrugged and glanced around. "Suit yourself, but there isn't much space anywhere else to sleep. What if I promise to stay on my side?"

"I know how long that would last," she grumbled, looking around the tiny bedroom. It held a desk with a straight chair that was definitely not conducive to sleep. There was little space on the floor. A dresser almost covered one wall. Night tables flanked the bed. An old television on a table stood in one corner, an addition long after she and her sister had moved away from home. A bookshelf took a lot of space. She didn't want to get into bed with Jake, but she didn't seem to have a choice.

She glanced at him as he tugged his shirt out of his pants. Muscles rippled in his back when he pulled off the shirt, tossed it on a chair and turned to face her. She tried to keep her gaze off his broad chest.

"What are you doing?" she asked.

"Stripping down for bed. I'm not sleeping in my clothes and then going to church in them."

"I'll bet you've never gone to church in a sports shirt like that in your life."

"Your mom said it was fine."

"You know you're just doing this to aggravate me," she said. She could see amusement dancing in his eyes. He unbuckled his belt and pulled it off.

"Don't you dare get naked."

"I wouldn't think of it," he said, looking as if biting back laughter. He eyed her. "As pretty as you look, don't you want to take off your clothes so they'll be presentable for church?"

"I'm not taking off my clothes and getting into bed with you," she flung at him as he stepped out of his trousers. Her pulse was jumping, speeding up with each garment he shed.

"Scared?" he asked softly. "Scared of what I'll do? Or are you afraid of what *you'll* do, Em?" he asked in a husky voice. He turned to look in the small closet for a hanger for his trousers. He was down to briefs, which hid little, and her mouth went dry. She was hot and the air in the room had vanished. She could barely breathe. He was taunting her.

"Jake, you know exactly what you're doing," she said in a low voice. His back was to her and her gaze ran over his muscles, his narrow waist, his tight bottom and long muscled legs. She saw two big bruises on his arm and shoulder and wondered if that was from the football. She whirled around, wiping her brow and breathing as if she'd run a marathon.

"Do you care which side of the bed you have?" he asked and this time she could clearly hear the amusement in his voice.

She clenched her fists. "No, dammit!" she flung at him, trying to figure out what to do. She could hear him rustling covers and tried to avoid imagining his muscled length stretched out between the sheets in her old bed, laughing and waiting for her to join him.

"I'd forgotten some of the definite advantages of a small bed," he said smugly.

Turning, she left the room and shut the door, hurrying to see if her mother was still up and she could borrow a robe. No light showed beneath her parents' bedroom door and she closed her eyes in frustration, then turned to go search the empty bedrooms. The closets were filled with scrapbooks, tools, all sorts of things. But no clothing.

She looked under the white chenille bedspread in one bedroom and in another at a second bare mattresses beneath a quilt, ready for clean sheets when someone came home for the night. She returned to yank off the chenille bedspread.

She took off her T-shirt and jeans and wrapped herself in the bedspread, giving the empty bed a longing look. But she didn't want to raise questions with her parents. Reluctantly, she returned to her room.

Jake was stretched out in bed, a sheet over his lower extremities, his bare chest and muscled stomach showing. He had his hands behind his head and a smile on his face that broadened when she appeared. "I thought perhaps you'd abandoned me for the night, but I'm happy to see you prefer my company to sleeping alone. And I do like your…whatever it is."

"Stop ogling me. I came back here so I wouldn't get a barrage of questions from my parents or get them worrying about our marriage. Time enough for that later," she added darkly, glaring at him. He had scooted to the far side of the bed and had a small night-light turned on. She switched off the overhead light.

"How can you expect me not to ogle you? You look luscious."

"Can you pull the sheet a little higher. I know you're not hot."

"*Au contraire,* darlin'," he drawled, rolling on his side and propping his head on his hand to look at her. "I'm hot as a pistol and you're the reason. You're wearing damn little and you're going to be in this bed in a minute—off limits to me, I know. The temperature in this bedroom is tropical."

"Jake, you're making everything harder." The minute the words were out of her mouth, she wished she could take them back.

"You couldn't be more wrong on that one!" He paused to give his words special emphasis. "You, darlin', are definitely the reason."

"You turn your back to me and stay on your side of the bed. Keep your hands to yourself," she said, thinking the night would seem a hundred hours long.

"I'll oblige, but you sound a little desperate. Is there some problem you're having difficulty dealing with?" he asked with innocence, his eyes dancing with mischief.

Her only problem was six feet two of masculinity, sexuality and incredible muscularity. A fantastic lover who could turn her inside out, make her lose control, envelope her in ecstasy. She wasn't about to tell him, though. His ego was big enough and she was certain none of her thoughts on his ability as a lover would vary a degree from his *own* opinion.

"Are you going to turn over?" she asked.

He waved a hand, smiled at her and turned so that his back was to her.

"I hope you're still wearing underwear," she said.

"Disturb you too much if I sleep in the buff?"

She glared at him and tried to ignore the images conjured up of him naked beneath the sheet. "Jake, can I get you to turn off the night-light?"

"If you don't mind, I need it in case I get up in the night and bump my shins."

Jake could move like a cat in the dark and he wouldn't be getting up, anyway. She glared at him and with a glance around the room and at the floor where she did not want to sleep, she lay down on top of the sheet and pulled another blanket over her.

"You'll get hot tonight, darlin'." His voice was a low rumble in the quiet room. "You're bound up like a mummy. If you get hot and kick off the sheet in your sleep, don't blame me."

The bed jiggled and she looked over her shoulder. "What are you doing?"

"Just turning over," he answered, holding up a bare muscled arm and waving his hand. "You're in bed now and covered to your chin."

"You're only inches away," she said between clenched teeth. "You stay on that side of the bed and keep your hands to yourself," she repeated, looking into eyes that smoldered with desire.

"I'll try to oblige, but until tonight, I've been accustomed to holding you in my arms while I sleep. Haven't you noticed that sometimes I pull you close when I'm sound asleep?"

"If you do that, I'll scoot away. Just don't do it when you're awake," she declared, wondering why she was even talking to him. Jake would do exactly as he pleased. She could detect a faint whiff of his aftershave, the special scent that was Jake.

"Wouldn't think of it. Too bad you're on the outs with me. My aching muscles could use a massage badly. I'm going to be too sore to move tomorrow."

Startled, she turned over to stare at him. "Are you telling me the truth?" she asked, recalling the bruises she'd noticed earlier.

"Darlin', I hurt from my neck to my toes. Particularly my lower back. That Anthony is short, but he's like a freight train. He tackled me and laid me out flat. And then they all piled on."

She bit her lip. She wouldn't put anything past Jake. He could be lying. Or he could be telling the truth. That gave he a twinge of guilt, since he'd been at the football practice be cause of her. She'd had no idea the guys would be so roug with him. Concerned, she looked at his bare shoulders an saw one dark bruise. "I never thought you'd get hurt. I'll hav a talk with them."

Jake grinned. "Hon, you skip the talk," he said. "I'll de with them."

She was certain Jake could take care of himself, but she talk to all four boys, anyway.

"Do you suppose your folks have any painkillers?"

"I'm sure they do in their bathroom, which I'd have to g to by going through their bedroom." She'd never known Ja to take any kind of pill. Nothing. She rubbed her forehea On one hand, she thought he deserved what he got. On t other, she felt badly about his injuries. She sat up and studi him more intently.

In the soft illumination of the night-light his mouth was invitation. She was aware of their breathing, the only sound the room. "Are you telling me the truth, or are you lying again

"I hurt, I promise you. But I'll live, so go on to sleep."

Her gaze raked over him and she saw another bruise on arm and a long scratch on his forearm.

"All right, Jake, but if you're lying again, so help me! Tu over. I'll give you a quick massage."

"Ahh, angel of mercy," he said with such satisfaction, sl wondered again whether he hurt at all, in spite of the bruise

She looked at his bare back and drew another deep breath. "Where do you hurt the most?"

"I don't believe you'll massage me there tonight," he answered.

"Jake, that does it!" she exclaimed, starting to turn away, but his hand snaked out and caught her wrist.

"Darlin', I'll behave. Give me a rubdown. My muscles are burning with pain."

She looked into eyes that told her nothing. "Show me where, Jake."

He rolled over on his stomach and pointed low on his back. "Down there the most. Then all the way up to my neck."

She glared at him, wondering again if she was falling for one of his tricks. She scooted closer and tried to give him a rub. His muscles were solid as rock and his body was warm. She was too aware of her hands on him, so close to his bottom. She looked at his thick black hair and remembered combing her fingers through it. Memories tormented her of showering kisses over his broad shoulders and down his smooth back. She tried to close her eyes and massage without thinking.

"Ahh, darlin'," he said in a husky voice. "Your hands are always magic. You don't know what you do to me."

"Save the conversation, Jake," she said. Touching him, looking at his bare back, made the erotic memories return. As she kneaded his back, the bedspread wrapped around her began to loosen. She slipped off the bed. He turned to look at her.

"What's wrong?"

"I'm coming around to the other side of the bed so I can reach you better."

"I could make a suggestion," he said.

"No." She imagined he would tell her to straddle him. She

wasn't doing that and she wasn't going to massage him much longer. He would just have to ache. She walked around the bed and he stretched back out on his stomach with his face turned toward her. Every stroke of her hands on his smooth warm skin was torment. Adding to her misery, reminding her of intimate moments, Jake closed his eyes, and made satisfied sounds—until finally she stood and went to her side of the bed. "That's it, Jake. Massage over."

"Thanks. I feel better," he said. He turned to watch her as she slid under the blankets, but stayed on top of the sheet to keep that slight barrier between them. He looked amused. "Scared to get under the covers with me, even when I promised I'd stay over here?"

"You're still only inches away. And stop talking. Good night, Jake." She clamped her mouth closed and squeezed her eyes shut and after a few minutes, realized she wasn't going to be able to sleep. She didn't want to give him the satisfaction of knowing that his presence disturbed her. She tried to breathe deeply, struggling to relax, but all she could do was listen to Jake's breathing and think how near his almost naked body was.

In spite of her anger, she sizzled with desire. How could she touch him, massage his back, look at his body in only briefs and not be aroused? She thought about taking a shower, but she'd have to go down the hall, and it would make noise that might wake her family. She gritted her teeth and attempted to relax, but failed as woefully as before.

She knew she was in for a sleepless night, hot with wanting Jake, angry and frustrated. How long would it be before she'd succumb to him? He had teased and flirted tonight, keeping her aware of him. He knew how seductive it was for her to see him bare and touch him and yet not be able to make love with him. She wanted his arms around her, wanted his kisses with a passion that equaled her anger.

She turned on her back, and it was hours before she finally drifted to sleep.

She awoke with Jake's arm around her and her leg thrown over him. She felt hard flat planes, sculpted muscles, crisp hairs tickling her breasts. Startled, she tried to scramble away. When his arm tightened, she looked up to meet his gaze.

"You promised..." she began.

"I woke up this way and I was afraid if I moved, I'd wake you."

"Right, Jake," she said, fuming, breathing hard, her skin tingling everywhere it made contact with his. Then she realized her blanket had gone and she was on top of the sheet, with only her lacy bra on, otherwise bare to her waist. She reached for a cover and yanked it up, glancing back at him. "Why don't you turn away?"

"I will if you want me to, but this view is the best in town," he said in a voice that strummed over her nerves like a caress.

She closed her eyes. "Turn your back."

He did and she stood, yanking up the spread to wrap herself in it. He glanced over his shoulder.

"Jake!" she snapped, turning her back.

"Can't blame me for sneaking a peek," he said. "I'm just looking, not touching. Or kissing. Or fondling—"

"Will you stop!" she hissed, and grabbed her clothes to go down the hall to the bathroom to shower and dress.

All through breakfast, she had to smile and be nice to Jake, who had caught on that she didn't want her parents to get an inkling about the true state of their marriage. Jake continually kept his arm around her, brushed feathery kisses on her temple, held her hand, as if they had just returned from an idyllic honeymoon.

She wasn't alone with him until she was in his car to drive to church. "You keep your hands to yourself the rest of the morning," she said.

"You said you didn't want your folks to know we're not happily married."

"You're fawning over me like we just got married and are wildly in love. You weren't like that after our honeymoon."

"Think back," he said. "I believe I might have been. Anyway, I'm just trying to present a picture of a happily wedded couple."

"Ease up a bit, please."

"Am I irritating you, or is it something else?"

"I'm not even going to answer that question," she replied in haughty tones. "I'll get over you, Jake. I promise I will."

He smiled at her and took her hand, but she shook free swiftly. "There's no one to convince right now. You stay on your side of the car."

"By the way, I actually had a good night's sleep. Your massage helped. I'm not as sore as I expected to be."

"I'm not sure I'm glad to hear that," she said.

"Wow," he teased. "Did someone get up on the wrong side of the bed? We could have remedied that."

She pressed her lips together and tried to ignore him.

During the church service, they shared a hymnal. She noticed that Jake knew the hymns without using the book and she wondered about his life growing up. They really knew very little about each other. She'd met his family, his mother and younger sister, but she didn't know them well. Jake didn't talk about his childhood much.

Once church and Sunday dinner were over, she and Jake left her parents' home in separate cars. She didn't want him to tease and flirt with her anymore today. She didn't want him looking for her, so she called home and left a message for him that she had errands to run and would be in late. She drove to the city library, curled up with a book, but she couldn't get past the first paragraph and finally dozed in the chair.

Her cell phone woke her and she saw the call was from Jake, but she ignored it and nodded off again. She got a cheese sandwich at a drive-through and finally went home, bracing herself for another encounter with Jake.

To her surprise, she didn't see him. His cars were in the garage and the limousine was there, so Jake had to be somewhere in the mansion, but she went to her room without seeing him.

She had no intention of going to look for him, certain that sooner or later he would appear.

When ten o'clock came, she changed and crawled into bed, exhausted and surprised she hadn't heard from Jake. She was worn-out emotionally and physically. She turned off the light, and rolled over and went to sleep, tormented by dreams of Jake holding her and kissing her.

Jake stood in the exercise room on the third floor and watched Emily drive into the garage. He knew she didn't want to see him, that there had been moments yesterday and today at her folks' when she'd been truly angry with him. But he also knew that she was angry at herself, too, because she couldn't resist responding to him.

And last night he couldn't resist flirting with her. She was too tempting. How he'd longed to unwrap that ridiculous bed-spread she put around herself and get rid of the wisps of lace, but he'd known he couldn't. He'd liked flirting with her and while he ached a little from football with the kids, he hadn't been in the dire shape he'd described to Emily, though he'd never admit it to her. Her hands on him had been both delight and torment. He liked her close, needed her touching him.

He'd been awake when he'd pulled her into his arms in bed. She'd been asleep, tousled, soft, warm, all curves and silky skin. When the six months were up, he didn't want her walking out on him.

He didn't even want this estrangement for the next six months. He rubbed his forehead. As far as he was concerned, every issue had a solution. Their relationship might have begun as a cut-and-dried contract, a business arrangement. But he wasn't sure that was all it was.

They were fabulous in bed, but nothing to each other otherwise. They weren't in love and never had been. She'd been sour on men and relationships when he'd proposed. He stood mulling over possibilities. He could court her, pour attention on her, win her heart. And then maybe in six months, she wouldn't walk out on him.

And with luck, it wouldn't take all six months to win her heart. Most women were easy. He'd just never really courted Emily or turned his full attention on her except in bed. He hit his forehead with his palm.

Where had his brain been? Why hadn't he courted his wife? He'd taken sex with her for granted because it was fabulous, but he'd disregarded everything else, all the attention women so dearly loved and would reciprocate tenfold.

That was the answer—he would go after Emily's heart. He

wanted to win her love. The sooner the better, because the quicker he could get her back in his bed, the greater the chances of getting a baby on the way…and Hub's money.

Whistling, Jake went to his bedroom where he made notations and reminders on his calendar. Why hadn't he thought of this before? He had no doubt he could win Emily's love.

They could start by having her family here more often. She'd have to associate with him when her family was around. He sat down to think of what would really please Emily and make an impression on her. First, he'd give her his undivided attention as much as possible. He'd work with those kids. He thought about how he could win them over. He wasn't going through another afternoon like yesterday. If he won their friendship, Emily would soften up tremendously.

Jake began to whistle again, wondering what she was doing now, planning on beginning his campaign in the morning. He intended to make his wife fall in love with him.

# Seven

Someone knocking on the door woke Emily, and she rolled over in bed, momentarily disoriented. Then she heard another soft rap.

"Come in," she called, pulling up the sheet even though she was dressed in blue silk pajamas.

Looking handsome and ready for the business world in a charcoal suit and white shirt, Jake entered and stood near the door. Her pulse jumped and for a moment she forgot the animosity between them, but then it returned and she stared at him, wondering what he wanted.

"I thought you'd be happy to know I'm going to Chicago. I'll return tomorrow. I'll try to contact the boys. If there's time we can squeeze in a practice during the week. I think it would be good for them."

"You do?" She was shocked that he actually was going to try to help them and put himself out more than she'd required.

"Yeah. But they're pretty busy and may not be able to, but we can get together for an hour and I can give them pointers."

"You're serious?" she asked, wondering what had brought this about.

He nodded. "I talked to your dad about working with them the other night, and it seemed like the thing to do."

She was surprised—and at a total loss.

"Bye, Em." He turned and left, closing the door behind him.

Emily felt as if she'd just had a dream, but she knew she was awake and it had all been real. That had been a man who looked like Jake, but didn't act like Jake. Jake wouldn't give the time of day to anyone unless they were family or friends, or he could benefit financially from the association. So what had brought about this extra time with the boys?

Remembering she had a busy day, she climbed out of bed. She was going to start spending Jake's first payment.

Thursday, the board of the children's shelter was meeting for her to talk to them about setting up a fund. Arranging things at her father's church would be easy, because the church committees and her dad would decide where the money would be spent, with a large portion going for missions.

She heard a car and hurried to the window in time to see the limo disappear around the curve of the drive. Today and most of tomorrow, Jake would be gone. Just like that. No flirting, no coming on to her. She rubbed her brow and wondered what had come over him. Maybe he had accepted everything and decided to make the best of it. Had her dad really changed Jake's view of the boys? She'd like to give her dad a call and see what she could get out of him on the subject, but her dad saved his words for his sermons. She might get a speech, but she didn't think he'd tell her what he and Jake discussed.

Hoping to look professional and businesslike, she selected a navy suit and white blouse.

She headed to a bank—not her usual one—and opened an account so she could transfer the money again before she made donations. She felt on thin ice in her volatile relationship with Jake, as if it could disintegrate completely at any time. She wanted to get this money distributed as swiftly as possible.

It was afternoon before she returned home, more relaxed to know that Jake was out of town. As she circled the sweeping drive, Emily wondered if she would ever become accustomed to his Texas mansion. It was far swankier than the island home, yet not as luxurious as his château in France with its formal gardens, fountains and antiques. She hadn't yet seen his New York condo or his home in the Colorado Rockies. She had no idea how large Jake's household staffs were and how many gardeners he employed, though she did know the head gardener at the Dallas mansion was Holz Ganshaw. Her husband was an enigma in many ways, and she suspected she might not know him or his lifestyle much better even after years of marriage—which wasn't going to happen, anyway.

With his first real taste of money, he'd retired his mother. Later, he'd provided for her lavishly and had sent his younger sister, Nina, to college. The gardeners and groundskeeper, along with his chauffeur, mechanic and bodyguard, all lived in quarters over the nine-car garage. Emily felt as if she was approaching a small village when she drove through the estate's tall wrought-iron gates.

When she entered the house, she went to the kitchen, to talk to Charley about her schedule for the week and to give him the rest of the day and Tuesday off. There were refrigerators and freezers filled with delicious food, and the walk-in pantry was like a small grocery.

"If you're certain you won't need me, Mrs. T.," Charley said, smiling as he got fresh bread out of an oven. His blue eyes were friendly and he always had a smile for her.

"I'll be fine," she assured him, accustomed to the staff addressing her as Mrs. T. At first she'd asked them to call her Emily, but no one would. When she was more insistent with Charley and Olive, Charley had started calling her "Mrs. T." and soon all the household staff followed his lead.

As she ascended the spiral staircase, she saw Olive's cheerful face, her brown eyes sparkling when she smiled. "Afternoon, Mrs. T. Glad to see you home. Can I get you anything?"

"No. But thanks, Olive."

"You had a delivery today. It's in the family room," Olive said, waving a plump hand. "I thought you might enjoy it more in there."

"A delivery?" Emily repeated.

"Yes, ma'am," Olive replied. "A very beautiful one," she added. "You go see."

Curious, Emily strolled into the family room. It was far less formal than the elegant living room, which was usually reserved for guests. As she entered the room with its high, beamed ceilings and fruitwood furniture, she gasped. On the polished cherry coffee table in front of one of the sofas, sat a vase with four dozen red roses and as many white tulips. The heady scent of flowers filled the air.

She crossed the room to open the card that sat on the table next to the vase. It read: "Look forward to coming home and seeing you." Jake had signed it in his familiar bold scrawl.

She was astonished. She hadn't expected to see much of

him from now on. At least, that was her plan. She looked at the card again and realized it wasn't *Jake's* plan. And why flowers? He'd never sent her flowers before.

Shrugging, she leaned forward to inhale deeply the rose scent. She touched a petal. Why flowers? Jake had a reason for everything he did and these blooms were spectacular.

"They're beautiful, ma'am," Olive repeated from the doorway.

"Yes, they are, but I expect to be out of the house a lot. Take them home with you, Olive, where you can enjoy them."

"Thank you, but I wouldn't dream of carrying away your beautiful flowers. I'll admire them in here."

Emily turned to look at the flowers again, still wondering why he'd sent them. She went upstairs to her bedroom and halted in surprise when she entered the room. Another huge bouquet of flowers sat in a vase on a table near the window. It was just as spectacular as the flowers downstairs. Her curiosity was heightened.

She crossed the room to open the card. "I know you have to go to church Wednesday night. But I hope you're free on Thursday. We both have to eat. Let me take you to dinner." It was signed, "Thinking of you, Jake."

She sat down to stare at the mix of daises, lilies, freesia, irises, carnations and dahlias and then studied the card again. Jake hoped to get her to go to dinner with him. That was what had brought on the flowers. Two mammoth, expensive bouquets was overdoing it, but that was Jake. If he wanted something, he went after it with total focus.

He could send her an entire garden, however, and he still could eat alone. She'd tell him to go find another woman. That should make him angry enough to send him on his way. Jake wasn't accustomed to failure. Pretty soon, she suspected, he'd want to be rid of her and any reminders of her or that he'd failed in an endeavor.

By eight that night she was curled in bed with a book when the phone rang. It was Jake. Lifting the receiver, she was thankful he was in Chicago.

"Hi, Jake. Thank you for the flowers. They're beautiful, but a bit much. If they're a bribe to get me to go to dinner with you Thursday night, it won't work. Sorry, but no."

"Have other plans?"

"Yes," she replied, even though she didn't.

"What are you doing now?"

"I'm reading," she said, trying to avoid conversation with him and get him off the line before she got pulled into doing something with him.

"You're in bed with a book," he said softly, and she wondered how he guessed when it was far earlier than she usually went to bed. "I'd like to be there with you," he said, lowering his voice another notch. "Last night was nice. And your massage helped take out the kinks," he added. "I wish you had your hands on me right now."

"Stop that," she said, setting aside her book.

"I invited your folks to come over for barbecue Saturday night."

"You did what? Jake, why? You've never invited them here before. What's the point now?" She knew the minute she asked. It enabled Jake to be with her. As long as he could be around her, he had a chance of winning her back and of her succumbing to his charm. Distance was her weapon, while proximity was Jake's. "Never mind," she said sharply.

"I also asked Will and Beth to come and bring their families. I told them it'll be casual and they can all swim. The kids will want to get into the pool."

She shook her head. "Very well. We don't need to chitchat, Jake. You've never called when you've been away on business before. No need to start now."

"Lighten up a little, Emily. I do have a reason for calling. I'm sorry, but I need a phone number that I left on the desk in my office. I hate to make you get out of bed, but can you go see if you can find it?"

She was tempted to refuse because she couldn't imagine anyone as efficient as Jake leaving behind a phone number that he would need. "I'll call you from downstairs," she said, and broke the connection, wondering if he had asked for the number to keep her on the phone so he could talk to her longer.

Flowers, a visit from her family, a long-distance phone call—all totally out of character for Jake. Also, his becoming so agreeable about coaching the boys. Jake was hell-bent on seduction. She had started down the winding stairs when she stopped, staring into space. Was he courting her, trying to make her fall in love with him?

Surprised, she continued to stare without moving, forgetting her purpose, her thoughts totally on Jake and his motives. If Jake wanted to win her heart, he would throw himself into charming her.

That had to be the reason for the flowers, the call, the invitation to her folks. Jake intended to win her love. And if she fell in love with him, he'd probably be able to talk her into staying with him. Anger surged, like a wave washing out and coming back in. Jake was still plotting to get his inheritance! He probably thought she would succumb to his charm if he threw himself into winning her love!

She descended the stairs slowly while she thought about this latest development. She could resist Jake, stay out of the house, keep busy and out of reach as much as possible for six months. There would be little he could do to win her favor. Yet she knew Jake—he'd figure out all sorts of reasons for them to be together, like inviting her family for barbecue.

She went to his office and found the number easily, then picked up the phone and called him back. She walked around to sit behind his elegant mahogany desk, and when Jake answered, she read the phone number to him.

"Thanks, Em. Sorry you had to get out of bed to get it. I should've tried to call you earlier, but I didn't think you'd already be in bed."

"That's all right, Jake. Have a nice night," she said, and hung up. As she did so, she heard his voice, but didn't care, idly wondering if he'd call her back with another excuse. She stared at the phone for a minute, deciding not to pick up if he did call.

She went back to her bedroom, but instead of getting into bed, she sat by the window, thinking about Jake, her fury growing. He was making another attempt to get his inheritance, trying to make her fall in love with him. She was certain he didn't care when he left a woman brokenhearted. She knew he'd done it plenty of times in the past. Seething, she was up until the early hours of the morning.

Tuesday, she made sizable donations, putting the money where Jake couldn't get it back. She no longer trusted him in the least.

Jake had lots of appointments, squeezing in as much as possible when he returned from Chicago on Tuesday so he could meet the four boys for a brief practice. He'd had his secretary contact each one of them. At six late that afternoon Jake changed into jeans and a T-shirt at the office and drove to the high-school football field. He'd had Charley pack a cooler and Toby, his chauffeur, take it to the office to put it in his car.

It was seven when he got out of the car and headed toward the four waiting boys. Jake had a football tucked under his arm.

"Hi," he said as he drew close, They mumbled greetings in return, but none rose to their feet. Jake stopped in front of them, looking each one in the eye.

"Look, I don't like this any more than you do, but we're all here because we like my wife," he announced. "So let's make an agreement here, just between the five of us," he said, seeing that he had their full attention for the first time. "We'll make it short. I have a car filled with food—hot pizzas, fried chicken and barbecued ribs. There's a cooler of soda. We'll toss the ball for about fifteen minutes, and then we'll eat and you can go. And we'll do it this way hereafter—if you can keep your mouths shut about it."

"Way to go, dude!" Orlando said, grinning and giving Jake a high-five as the others got up and murmured approval.

"Okay," Jake said, glancing at his watch. "Spread out and we'll toss a few and practice some kicking."

They threw the ball for about five minutes and then they tried to kick field goals through rickety wooden posts that had long ago lost their paint. They got interested in Jake's instructions.

When the ball left his hands, Jake glanced at his watch and saw it had been exactly fifteen minutes.

"Guys, it's time to eat," he said, running and reaching out to catch a high, spiraling pass from Orlando. "Good one," he said and received a grin as the four men gathered balls and approached him.

"You guys go get the food," Jake said. Fishing in his pocket, Jake pulled out his keys and tossed them to Anthony who caught them easily.

"Hey, man, you given' us your keys? We might take a joy-ride. I've never driven a Jag," he said and grinned.

Laughing, Jake shook his head. "Just get the food. It's a car and goes like other cars."

"Yeah, right," Anthony replied, striding off with the others.

Jake turned away to gather equipment. He trusted all four boys and knew they were too smart and too honest to take his car. He felt invigorated from the workout and realized he'd enjoyed it and the guys had relaxed and cooperated.

In minutes they were back and unpacked all the food as they sat one the bleachers and began to eat pizza and ribs.

"Tell us about the old days and when you played ball," Orlando said. "What position did you play?"

Jake grinned and figured this is when they'd give up on his coaching. "The years I played, I was the field goal kicker."

"No kiddin'?" Anthony asked and Tanek stopped eating.

"Was it difficult to get that position?" Tanek asked and Jake shook his head.

"Not really."

"What kind of record did you have?" Anthony asked, surprising Jake that they were interested.

Jake shrugged. "Good enough to stay on my scholarship."

"C'mon, man, what was your record?" Orlando persisted, and the others chimed in.

"Thirty-six of thirty-eight field goals. I had four fifty-yard field goals," Jake said, reciting figures from college days and realizing all four guys had stopped eating to listen.

"What awards?" Orlando asked and all of them listened attentively as Jake listed some, growing even more surprised by the depth of their interest. They continued eating, but were filled with questions and when they finished, as they packed up the remains, Tanek turned to Jake.

"Have time for another round of practice, Jake?"

Startled, Jake paused and realized all of them were waiting for his answer. "Sure. If you guys want to, it's fine with me. We can put the food in the car when we leave. Grab the balls."

They were still at it when the sun went down, and finally had to stop for the night. When Jake learned that the boys all walked home, he had them put the cooler in the back of his car and gave them all rides, along with the leftovers.

As he drove home, he was surprised at himself and what had transpired at the practice. Once the boys knew that they didn't have to work with him and that he was only doing this to please Emily, they relaxed and got friendlier. So did he. And, he had to admit, he'd enjoyed himself. They even played tag football for a while. It had been the first time he'd done that in years, but it had sure felt good.

He shook his head, wondering if Emily would be happy about his bonding with the boys. Would she even believe him? Or care?

His marriage had taken a nosedive, but he intended to court her every way he knew how to try to win her affections. A helluva lot was at stake. He wanted this as much as he'd ever wanted anything in his life.

Last night had been good—sleeping in the same small bed with her had been as good as it could get without getting sexual. All the flames of her anger couldn't burn away the response she had to him.

He was eager to get home and tell her that he had bonded with the boys. He wondered if that would take away a degree of her anger with him.

Tuesday evening Emily went to dinner with a friend to avoid Jake and slipped into the house late and as quietly as possible, hurrying to her room and closing the door.

She could elude Jake until Saturday night when her family was coming, but she suspected he would try everything possible to get time with her. Determined to thwart him, she decided to stay out of the house as much as possible.

Early Wednesday morning, she heard a car and looked out to see the limousine headed down the drive. So Jake had gone for the day. She was relieved, certain he hadn't given up hope on his inheritance.

That day, more flowers arrived, and she prevailed on Olive to take two bouquets home. As Jake's usual style was going at something wholeheartedly, she thought the mansion, as big as it was, would look like a florist's shop before long.

Emily left early in the afternoon for errands and to avoid seeing Jake before she left for church and her tutoring commitments.

Thursday morning she ate breakfast away from home, before a meeting at the children's shelter. As she rushed to get there on time, she congratulated herself on her success in evading Jake.

When she entered the conference room at the children's shelter, Jake rose from a chair and smiled at her.

Shocked, she halted, hating that her pulse raced as swiftly as ever at the sight of him. She smiled and greeted everyone perfunctorily, not seeing them as she looked at Jake.

Dressed in a gray suit, he appeared relaxed and in charge.

Her throat tightened. Taking a deep breath, she crossed the room to him, tingling from head to toe as his gaze drifted slowly down and then back up over her, taking in every inch.

"What are you doing here?" she asked.

"Good morning," he said. Softly so only she could hear he added, "Because of the money you've donated—they think it's actually from both of us and they're grateful, Surely, you don't mind?"

She inhaled and shook her head, wanting to avoid admitting to him that she didn't want him around. He would know why. All he had to do was detect her out-of-control pulse and he'd get that satisfied look. She wanted to cry in frustration, except she wasn't going to give him the satisfaction.

"You look absolutely gorgeous," he murmured, running his hand beneath the collar of her suit. His knuckles brushed her throat and she gulped for air.

"Have you contributed all you're going to to this cause, or will there be more donations later?" he asked.

"I'm saving the rest of the money for other charities," she answered, still shocked to find him here.

The chairman and two other board members came to greet Jake and she couldn't get away politely. Jake took her arm, standing close beside her, sliding his hand down to her wrist. He could feel her pulse and knew that her anger with him didn't run deep enough to kill that intense physical response to him.

"Now that we're all here, we might as well be seated," the chairwoman said in her high lilting voice.

Jake pulled out a chair for Emily and then sat close beside her. The shelter was a not-for-profit organization. It ran on a shoestring and she wondered what Jake thought of the small conference room.

When the chairwoman got to Jake's introduction, she gave both Emily and Jake a fervent thank-you for the generous donation to the shelter. "In addition, after the meeting, Mr. Thorne has offered to take the board to lunch, so we'll all adjourn to Baker's," she said, naming a restaurant with excellent cuisine, but more than six miles from the shelter.

Emily met Jake's gaze. She would be eating lunch with him. She wondered if all this had come about because she had turned him down for dinner tonight.

After the board meeting, Jake managed with polite finesse to see to it that Emily, and only Emily, was in his car for the drive to Baker's.

As soon as he slid behind the wheel and they drove away, she remarked dryly, "You've developed an interest in the shelter."

"I'm pursuing another interest. You," he said, glancing at her.

"At least you're truthful about it. Should I expect to see you at all my charities now?"

One corner of his mouth tugged up. "Is that prospect good or bad?"

Her patience snapped. But instead of flinging the retort she wanted, she leaned over, close to him, taking advantage of the fact that he was driving and had to keep his attention on the road and his hands on the wheel. "Darlin'," she said in a breathy voice, running her hand along his thigh, "I'm just delighted to have you take all this interest in me and my projects. It's so flattering, Jake, to know you'd give your time this way." She leaned closer to kiss his cheek.

He inhaled sharply. "Dammit, Emily, you make me want to ditch lunch and find a hotel room."

Smiling at him, she sat back, enjoying the effect she had on him when he could do nothing about it. "Sorry, hon," she said with a stab of vengeful satisfaction, "but we're not getting a hotel room and we do have to show up for lunch. After all, you offered to buy for the entire board."

"What about after lunch?"

"I have an appointment at the hairdresser. But you know I wouldn't go to a hotel room with you, anyway."

"And you're busy tonight."

"That's right," she replied sweetly. A muscle worked in his jaw and she felt even better. His presence disturbed her and his light touches stirred desire that she couldn't combat. But if she was going to be on fire with wanting him, he could suffer a little frustration in return.

Suddenly, inspiration struck, and she knew how to fight Jake's seduction campaign.

# Eight

Emily was certain Jake would appear everywhere she couldn't protest against his presence publicly. There was no way to avoid him. Not if he was determined to get into her life as much as possible. Between her projects, her family and living under the same roof, she would see him often and he would be his most charming, she was sure.

But at the very least, she could tease him, turn him on and shut him down. And there was nothing he could do about it. He was unaccustomed to frustration, particularly where women were concerned. If he intended to try to seduce her, he could just suffer a little himself.

She couldn't see any danger he would actually fall in love with her—he was too wound up in himself. But he could get back some of the frustration he was causing her.

Smiling at him, she turned to study him. "It's nice of you to take the board to lunch. They'll appreciate it."

"You know I want to be with you," he answered.

"That makes my heart race," she said, placing her hand on his leg lightly.

He glanced at her again. "You're not angry? I got the feeling that you were unhappy I showed up at the shelter."

"I just told you, I'm glad to see you take an interest in my projects. It's very flattering, Jake."

His eyes narrowed and he studied her briefly before he had to turn his attention back to his driving.

"I heard you invited my entire family to dinner Saturday night—that's also great. You've never taken that much interest in them before, either."

"I should have, Em," he said easily. "I enjoyed being with them Saturday night and Sunday. I've never had a family like yours. You should be thankful for them."

"I am. I know I have a great family and I love all of them. And I'm glad two of my siblings live here. I wish they all did. Enjoy them while you can," she said lightly, looking out the window. They arrived at the restaurant and Jake draped his arm across her shoulders as they walked in.

Again, Jake sat beside her, but he gave his attention to those around him. He had them laughing at his amusing anecdotes, becoming the center of attention.

On the way back to pick up her car, she shifted to face him. "You won all of them over. They think you're the most delightful person. I bet they want to ask you to join the board."

"You don't know that."

"They told me how much they liked you, each one of them, before we left. They all appreciated the lunch."

"I was glad to do it. Nice people, Emily. I have to admit I was surprised by how few kids they've been able to keep there."

"With your money, they'll be able to double the number of children and hire more qualified staff. The money is truly wonderful, Jake. That's twenty little kids we're getting off the street."

A muscle worked in Jake's jaw. She wondered if she should have been telling him more about her projects all along. Yet she knew that earlier, he probably wouldn't really have listened to her or thought about what she was telling him.

"Your money will be fabulous for them. For Dad's church, as well. A lot of it will go to mission trips and help people all over the world."

"You have a big heart, Em," he said.

She took his hand and brushed his knuckles with her lips. "Thanks to you and your generosity."

He inhaled and shot her a quick glance. "Go out to dinner with me Friday night."

It was on the tip of her tongue to refuse, but then she recalled her intentions to torment him. "Actually, my plans have changed. I can go tonight," she said.

He gave her another quick surprised glance and she was glad to see that he was puzzled by her change of heart. "Excellent! How's seven?"

"Fine with me," she said softly. "As you said, we both need to eat. I'm going to dinner with you, but no dancing. Make no mistake—nothing changes about our agreement."

He nodded and this time his expression was shuttered, the questioning expression gone. "Fine. I do understand. As long as that's what you want, I'll stick with it."

He dropped her at the shelter, where she picked up her car and left for her appointment at the hairdresser's. Then she intended to buy a new dress to wear tonight.

At ten minutes before seven, she took one last long loo
in the mirror. Her hair was swept back from both sides of he
face and pinned to fall freely at the back of her head.

She had on a bit more makeup than usual and wore th
diamond-and-sapphire necklace Jake had given her. It caugh
the light and sparkled. Her perfume was new, a slightly les
sweet scent than she usually wore.

And then there was her dress. The red charmeuse dress wa
sleeveless, with a low-cut back and draped neckline. It ende
just below her knees and the fabric clung to her figure. He
feet were in high-heeled red sandals.

Deciding she was ready to join Jake, she picked up he
purse and went downstairs.

She found him in the conservatory, talking on his ce
phone. He turned to look at her as he hung up. He gave her
thorough perusal.

As he crossed the room to her, she smiled. "I'm ready to go

"You look fantastic, Em," he said in a raspy voice
"Beautiful!"

"Thank you. You look nice yourself."

He placed warm hands on her shoulders, making her hea
flutter. "What's brought about the thaw in our relationship
You're not burning with fury like you were."

"I've adjusted to the situation," she replied with a shrug
"You've given me a sizable amount to spend on my projec
and you seem interested in them. There's no point in holdin
a grudge. Maybe I've lived with you long enough to catc
your optimism."

"It's great, but I'm surprised. You never cease to surpris
me. I can't take anything for granted with you."

"Some things you can. I'll stick by what I've agreed," she sai

He nodded, but she noticed tiny beads of perspiration on his brow. She wanted to laugh with satisfaction, yet she knew better than to think she'd gotten the best of Jake. He had far more practice at being shrewd and cunning than she had.

"Any time you change your mind, just say the word. I want you in the worst way." His voice was almost a whisper.

"You do make me feel desired, Jake. And important to you beyond your need to become a father. But I know that's the only reason."

"No, it's not," he said. He reached out to caress her arm, a feathery touch that increased the tension.

"Shall we go?" she said. "It's been a long time since lunch."

He continued to study her, reaching up to twirl a long lock of hair around his finger while he caressed her nape with his other hand. Tingles spiraled and need mushroomed, but she didn't want to let him know, so she stood still, watching him, her heart pounding as his gaze drifted to her mouth.

"Yes, let's go," he agreed, taking her arm.

He escorted her to the car and opened the door for her, stepping back to let her to climb in.

"Em," he said, his voice raspy again.

Turning to look at him, she saw the scalding heat in his eyes. Once again, he grasped her shoulders lightly and turned her away from him. He ran his finger down her bare back, sending sizzles streaking through her system that heated her and fueled hungry longing for Jake's lovemaking.

"Jake," she cautioned, facing him quickly and wishing she could squelch the heat.

"That dress isn't like you," he said gruffly. "It screams seduction."

"It does no such thing," she said, hoping she sounded

matter-of-fact and hating the breathlessness she detected in her reply. "It's expensive. I liked the way it fit."

"I'm not complaining," he said, studying her intently now. Her heart thudded. Had she gone too far too quickly? Well, if she disturbed him too much, Jake could leave her at home and go eat alone.

"Fine," she answered blithely. "Let's go get dinner." She sat in the car and looked up expectantly. He closed the door and went around the car, and again, she knew she was walking a tightrope and could come tumbling down at any moment. Jake was a master of seduction. Charismatic and mesmerizing, he could weave a web of magic that made her will melt. She stared straight ahead, waiting for her racing heart to slow and for erotic images to stop tormenting her.

As long as she flirted and toyed with him, she'd also have to struggle to resist him.

"Penny for your thoughts," he said, taking her hand and winding his fingers through hers.

She moved both of their hands to his warm thigh, placing her hand against him and watching his chest expand as he inhaled.

"You and I can arouse each other so easily. We'd do better if we didn't spend time together," she said.

He shook his head. "I like to be with you. You're still my wife. Torment or not, things are better when we're together."

"Fine. I'm glad we can be civil to each other."

He took her to an elegant steakhouse. They sat by a floor-to-ceiling window that overlooked one of Dallas's lakes and she could see sailboats in the distance. Adding to the inviting ambiance was a ballad played softly on a piano across the room.

She ordered her usual water and Jake a martini and then

turned her attention to the menu that had been placed in front of her. She took her time, finally closing it and looking around, aware Jake was sipping his drink, watching her.

She smiled at him. "You've turned all the women's heads, as usual. I think I married the most handsome man in Texas."

"A lot of good it's doing me. Thanks, anyway," he said. "I suspect they were looking at your dress in the way women do when they see something they wish they'd bought. It's gorgeous, Em."

"Thank you. You said it isn't typical of me. Perhaps I'm changing—your influence."

"You're giving me credit for something I didn't do. Speaking of influence, I had another practice with the guys this week on Tuesday night."

"I know. Wednesday night I saw Orlando at church and he told me. He was impressed with your football knowledge. You're living up to my expectations with them," she said, smiling over her glass of water.

"That's surprising, but they all paid attention. Tanek is a decent kicker. He has potential."

"I'll count on you to bring out the best in them," she said cheerfully.

"See, Em, you *can* count on me. Don't say you can't ever trust me. Sometimes I can give you just what you expect."

"Or much more than I dreamed possible," she drawled softly, leaning forward over the table. His chest expanded as he stared at her. "Beyond my wildest expectations," she added in a sultry drawl.

He appeared to gulp for air. "Em, what the hell are you doing? You're flirting."

"Is that a complaint, Jake?"

He watched her like a tiger eyeing meat. Suddenly, he smiled. "Could it be you're fighting fire with fire, and trying to give me some of my own back?"

"Jake! You know me better than that. Maybe your flowers have thawed me a little," she protested, but her heart thumped, her palms became sweaty, and she realized she shouldn't have been so blatant in her willingness to be with him.

He grinned. "I've decided, in spite of the years since we first met, I don't know you at all. And the florists' entire supply of posies wouldn't thaw you one degree if you were truly angry with me."

"Make no mistake, here. I am truly angry," she said quietly. "When we get back to the house, you'll go your way and I'll go mine."

He sipped his martini and looked at her over the rim of his glass. She wondered what he was thinking.

"So I mustn't flirt with you," she said, leaning forward once again and smiling at him.

"That's definitely not what I said, darlin'," he drawled, leaning forward, too. He reached out to caress her cheek lightly. She tingled and wondered if she had chosen the wrong strategy. Yet it served Jake right and she suspected she was getting to him.

"It's too bad, Jake. Talk about potential—we had a lot going for us that could have led to a happy marriage."

"It's not over yet and all isn't lost," he said. "Your eyes are beautiful, Em." He took her hand, but she pulled it away and sat back in her chair.

"It isn't over, but it's definitely lost."

"I gave you some negotiation advice—which, incidentally, you took to heart. Now I'll give you some more—don't give up on an agreement prematurely. Look for the possibilities. Enjoy what works," he added huskily. "You know there's one area between us that does satisfy both of us, totally. You might rethink giving it up."

She smiled. "Even if I go on the pill."

She saw the brief flicker in his eyes and knew she'd scored a direct hit. Jake obviously hadn't thought about birth control. She watched him keep his iron control while he mulled over the best way to handle this new threat.

"Pill or no pill," he said, reaching over to take her hand firmly this time. "Since we said our vows, there has never been a time I didn't want to make love to you. That hasn't changed." He raised her palm to his lips to trail kisses across it.

Her temperature climbed. Alarm bells went off in her mind—what had she gotten herself into? An evening of Jake's total attention with seduction his sole aim. Withdrawing her hand, she gazed at him. "While you tempt me, I won't run that risk. My emotions are too tied up. When you caress and kiss me all over my body and I kiss you all over yours," she said in a breathy voice, "*you* can remain emotionally detached. But my emotions are entangled in every stroke and kiss."

He stared at her impassively, but she saw tiny beads of perspiration pop out on his forehead and knew she was getting to him.

He smiled slightly, a faint tug of one corner of his mouth. "You're conjuring up fiery images, Em. Are you trying to ruin my sleep tonight?"

"Imagine what you will. I'm just stating a fact."

The waiter arrived with their salads and Emily turned her attention to her food, relieved to get even a slight reprieve from their conversation. She was conscious of Jake, though, watching her and wrapped up in his own unfathomable thoughts.

Through dinner and the drive home, they continued flirting with each other. Jake shed his jacket and tie and unbuttoned the neck of his shirt. He looked sexy and approachable and too appealing for her to say good-night and walk away. Yet she knew she was going to have to. And quickly.

Emily's pulse drummed. She had flirted all evening with Jake. Now she wanted to go to her room and close the door, but she suspected it wouldn't be that simple. Jake wasn't accustomed to a woman flirting with him and then brushing him off.

The last part of the drive she grew quiet and he noticed.

"Cat got your tongue?" he asked.

"I suppose. Thank you for a delicious dinner."

He smiled. "Go with me again tomorrow night."

"Let's eat at home. We have everything we could want here."

"Good idea. I'll grill whatever you'd like—steaks, chicken, fish, shrimp."

He parked at the back entrance, coming around to open her door. He took her arm and walked with her in silence to the house. When he stopped to switch off the alarm, she hurried ahead.

"Night, Jake," she called over her shoulder.

She heard his footsteps, and then his hand closed on her arm. "Em," he said as he turned her around.

One look in his stormy gray eyes and her heart thudded. The moment was electric. Lightning might as well have been streaking the room and she could practically hear thunder booming. She couldn't breathe.

His gaze lowered to her mouth. "You've tormented me with hot images all evening long. You look good enough to eat," he said, combing pins out of her hair and sending them flying. Her pulse was pounding, roaring in her ears, and she couldn't conjure up a protest.

"Dammit, you asked to be kissed!" he said. His mouth covered hers, hard, his tongue sliding into her mouth possessively as he wrapped a strong arm around her waist and pulled her up against him.

She couldn't stop him. He leaned over her, his arm holding her, his other hand sliding slowly down her back, down over her bottom and the back of her thigh. He turned slightly and his hand drifted over her breast, rubbing her nipple.

Clinging to him, she moaned. She had to stop him soon, but she wanted his kisses desperately. He was aroused, enticing, irresistible. And the worst person for her to become intimate with. If she did, all was lost.

Her negative thoughts were fleeting, dim and fuzzy. They nagged at her as she returned his kisses passionately. She clung to him and knew she was building fires she couldn't control.

She pushed against his chest lightly and then with more force.

He released her slightly and they both gasped for breath. "It isn't fair you can do this to me," she whispered.

"What isn't fair is the way you've teased and flirted all evening. You're not walking away from that. Not yet," he said, dipping his head for another long, passionate kiss that was even more scalding than before.

This time when she pushed against his chest, she twisted out of his arms. "You have to stop, Jake! I'm not going to let you seduce me. I've flirted, but you're the one who asked me to dinner. You don't have to take me out. But if you do, you know what our agreement is. I'm not going to bed with you!" she flung at him, her fists clenched, fighting the desire threat-

ening to consume her. His black hair fell over his forehead as
he fought for breath. His partially unbuttoned shirt tempted
her. She wanted to yank it off him and feel his bare chest
against her bare skin.

With a cry she turned and rushed to the back of the house
to put some distance between them.

To her relief, he didn't follow her. She closed the door to
a downstairs bedroom and leaned against it. She sizzled with
wanting Jake. His kisses were fantastic and she wanted to
make love with him all night long. She rubbed her forehead
and knew she was going to have to go back to avoiding him.
She couldn't flirt and spend time with him without needing
him more than ever.

She didn't want to see him again tonight and so took the
long way back to her room. The door to his bedroom stood
open and the room was dark, so Jake was obviously elsewhere. She rushed to her room and closed the door. Sleep
wouldn't come for hours.

She was still on fire with wanting him. Six months from
now would she be able to walk out of this life and leave Jake?
He had charmed her tonight, almost kissed her into submis-
sion, made her want him with all her being. She thought about
Hubert Braden's letter and Jake's deception, how enraged
she'd been. She dredged up that anger and pulled it around
her like a tattered coat in a blizzard.

She stripped down and showered, staying under the spray
a long time, wishing she could wash away memories.

Afterward she dried herself, pulled on silk pajamas and
wrapped herself in a thick terry robe. She climbed into bed
and turned on a movie she never saw. Since he'd invited her
family for dinner, Saturday night, she'd have to play the

devoted wife. But she wasn't going out to dinner with Jake again this week. If she did, she might not be able to resist falling into his bed.

Saturday she vowed she would occupy herself with her family and keep Jake at a distance. Six months was an eternity. She wondered whether she'd make it through the weekend without succumbing to him.

# Nine

Jake had hired caterers, so there was little for Emily to do on Saturday. She spent the afternoon getting ready and with each minute that passed, her tension and anticipation mounted. She hadn't been able to shake the desire for Jake that had consumed her since Thursday evening. She had avoided him, but not seeing him hadn't put out the fires he'd started.

She was ready too early, studying herself critically. She wore jeans and a beige knit shirt and had tied her hair back with a silk scarf. Surveying herself in the mirror, she thought she was plainly dressed. She didn't want to look too enticing to Jake.

A knock on her door startled her and she whirled around, knowing it was Jake. She was tempted to not even answer. "Come in," she said at last.

He opened the door and was as devastating as she'd expected. The jeans he wore were tight and low on his narrow hips, emphasizing long legs that looked even longer now that he was wearing boots. His pale-blue knit shirt clearly revealed his muscles. He looked fit and filled with vitality.

His gaze raked her slowly. "You look as gorgeous as always," he said as if there was no conflict between them. He placed his hands on her shoulders. "This should be fun. I don't know why we haven't had your family over more." Before she gave him the cynical answer that popped into mind immediately, he continued, "Em, I invited the kids I coach. I thought you'd like to have them here."

She stared at him, at a loss for words.

"Is that all right with you?" he asked, jolting her out of her daze. She blinked at him.

"Of course it is. I'm just amazed that you'd do such a thing."

"As I told you things have improved."

"Oh, Jake! I knew you could do it!" she exclaimed without thinking, thrilled that he had bonded with the boys. She threw her arms around his neck and hugged him. "Thank you so much! It's important to me and wonderful for them! I'm so grateful—" She knew she was babbling, but she was bubbling with excitement, thrilled over this turn of events and excited for the boys. Finally, she'd found the goodness in Jake she'd felt was there all the time, just buried beneath ambition and drive.

Instantly, his arm banded her waist and he leaned down. She looked up at him and his mouth covered hers, ending the conversation. His tongue thrust slowly into her mouth, deep and stroking, lighting fires in her. Jake leaned over her, his tongue thrusting slowly, taunting and teasing.

She was drowning in the kiss. It had been over a week since they'd made love, a week with Jake doing everything in his power to please her if he'd had the chance. A week with nights together—at her parents' and then at dinner—in which he'd flirted and teased and charmed, inflaming her desire until it was a constant scalding blaze.

Now with his kiss, she was momentarily lost, spinning away into a raging bonfire of need. Her hands roamed hungrily over him, trailing down over his tight jeans and then back up to tug his shirt up, run her hands across his chest and tangle her fingers in his chest hair. Time and circumstances splintered into nothing. Her anger melted. Desire consumed her.

Jake yanked out her shirt, pulled it over her head and tossed it away. As he continued kissing her, her bra fell away and he cupped her breasts. His thumbs circled her nipples, making her moan with pleasure, the sound lost in their kisses.

She felt his hands at the waist of her jeans, but she was only dimly aware of them until her jeans slid down. His fingers crept between her thighs to find her feminine bud and rub her until she was beyond turning back.

She heard the jingle of his belt buckle and then felt his thick rod against her belly. She pushed away his briefs, not caring when or how his jeans were moved out of the way.

Taking her with him, Jake kicked the door closed, settled back against it and lifted her. She shook her jeans from her feet, reaching down to tug off her lace panties. Then she wrapped her legs around him while he braced himself against the wall. He lowered her to his thick rod and she cried out with pleasure, biting his neck lightly, showering kisses along his cheek to his mouth.

He thrust into her and desire was white-hot, consuming her. He groaned and moved his hips faster, as she plunged and gyrated with him. Tension wound tighter, bright lights exploding behind her eyes, sensations battering her.

Her climax came as he thrust frantically with his own and they shuddered together. Ecstasy enveloped her. She relaxed on him, release and rapture still shrouding her while she kissed his broad shoulder. "Jake," she whispered, wondering if she could be falling in love.

She ran her hands over him, wanting to love again, knowing she had found release and satisfaction that was fleeting and would only make her want more. She wanted to make love with him all night long. Yet her feelings hadn't changed about his deception and greed.

She looked up at him to find him watching her. He leaned down to kiss her again, long and thoroughly. When he raised his head, he shifted her to let her slowly slide down and stand on her feet.

"Later," he said solemnly, "we'll finish what we started. You have no idea what you do to me," he added, brushing kisses on her temple before releasing her. "Let's clean up. I'll see you downstairs."

He grabbed his clothes. As he reached for the door handle, she held her clothes in front of her. "Jake…" He paused to look at her.

"Thanks for inviting the boys tonight," she said. "I'm pleased beyond measure."

One corner of his mouth quirked up. "We're making progress, Em," he said. "Later." He left and she stared at the door.

"Damn you, Jake. Why do you have these moments when you do something I can't resist?" she asked the empty room.

She wondered if he'd invited the boys just to please her. Whether he had or not, it meant he truly was working with them and getting to know them. Exhilaration bubbled and made her laugh with pleasure, but it also raised Jake in her esteem, something she didn't want to happen. Her heart was definitely in danger—Jake was beginning to do things that made her happy, things that brought out the goodness in his heart.

Her body tingled from Jake's loving, too. She'd never intended for that to happen again, but when he kissed her she hadn't wanted to stop.

She hurried to shower and dress all over again in fresh clothes before rushing downstairs.

The tall French doors in the loggia were open to the veranda. Jake already stood there, talking to the event planner and caterer. The veranda was beautiful as always. It needed almost nothing changed for the party except a few more tables. The tangy smell of barbecue wafted through the air and tiny wisps of smoke escaped from the enormous stainless steel grill.

Jake left the caterer to meet her and her heart skipped. His gaze was warm, filled with desire. She saw that their frantic lovemaking had stirred up a storm, instead of calming things. His eyes lit up as he reached out.

"That was fabulous, Em," he said. "But I want more. I can take you to far greater heights than we had time for upstairs."

"I didn't intend for that to happen," she whispered, unable to get that barrier back around her heart.

"It was amazing," he said. "Every time I look at you tonight, I'll think about it. I want to take all night with you." He untied the scarf that held her hair and drew it away slowly across her nape. "I like your hair better *this* way," he said. "Makes me want to run my hands through it."

She shook her head. "Jake, I don't want to go back to sharing the same room. Not yet. Let's not get into all that right before everyone arrives."

"Fine with me," he said, looking at her mouth.

"Jake…" She licked her lower lip and then wished she hadn't.

He leaned down to kiss her. It was a slow lingering kiss that made her heart pound.

She pushed against his chest. "Jake, we're not alone. My family will be here any minute," she whispered.

"Why shouldn't I kiss my wife? You look sexy tonight. I like your jeans."

She could say the same to him, but she wasn't going to. "Thank you." She glanced around. "It still seems weird to have a dinner party and not have to do anything to get ready."

"I'd think you'd like it." He looked over her head. "Here comes your family." Jake took her arm as they went to greet everyone.

Jake's butler, Terry, showed her parents in. Her smiling father gave her a hug and a kiss and then turned to shake hands with Jake while she hugged her mother.

Soon the rest of her family arrived, the children running to give Emily a hug and quick reserved greetings for Jake before they clamored for their parents to take them in the pool. Trish, her oldest niece, was five and knew how to swim. In minutes, Trish was in the shallow end, swimming back and forth. While her dad, brother and brother-in-law stood talking to Jake, the mothers and the other two children got into the pool, the kids squealing with joy. Emily joined her mother on a chaise longue to watch her nieces and nephew.

As she chatted with her mother, she glanced across the veranda and met Jake's gaze. She felt an electric jolt. Even across the veranda, his look said he wanted her, and she tried to draw a long breath, feeling as if the air had vanished around her. She guessed he was thinking about their lovemaking.

She turned away, trying to concentrate on watching the kids splash in the pool and forget her long-legged husband in his tight jeans. But she couldn't.

Jake and the other men stood in a cluster talking, cold beers in hand. Her gaze ran over her husband and her heart drummed. Tonight had been a special gift. Having her family and the boys over for barbecue meant everything, because it was sincere. For a few minutes, while giving herself to Jake, she had lost all animosity toward him. She knew she should be more cautious, but it had been impossible to stop.

The boys arrived and she was happy to see they looked scrubbed and dressed nicely. Anthony and Orlando both wore knit shirts, while Tanek and Enzo wore plaid cotton shirts. All four wore jeans that for once, weren't ripped or ragged.

She went to greet them, shaking hands with each. "I'm so glad you're here. Come with me and I'll introduce you to my family. Later, get the kids to give you a tour of the house. There's a room with video games and a pool table."

"Some house, Mrs. Thorne," Anthony said.

"I'm surprised your husband gives us even one minute of his time," Orlando added, glancing around. "If I had all this, I doubt if I'd spend time with a bunch of poor kids."

"I think you would. You already take time to work with younger kids. Just don't forget that when you're out of school and working. Someone helped Jake once upon a time."

Orlando's blue eyes met hers and he nodded solemnly. "I guess you're right. He's a cool dude." He looked over her head at the mansion. "This is really something. Biggest home I've ever been in."

"It's big, but it's comfortable," she said.

She introduced them to the men and then took them to

meet the rest of her family before telling them to go get something to drink. In a few minutes she glanced over at the group of males and was relieved to see that all four boys had cans of soda. She wondered if they'd avoided beer for her sake or because, for Orlando and Anthony, their minister was present. Or had Jake only offered them soda? Whatever the reason, she was glad.

"Some party, sis. It's a fun evening," Will said, walking up to her as she was pouring more water into her glass. "The boys said Jake is coaching them."

"Yes. You should join them. I think Jake's beginning to enjoy it."

"He told me to come out," Will said, surprising her. "I might do it. I could use the exercise."

"You used to play, but be careful. Jake works out and he said those boys are strong and fit." Her brother shrugged, and she knew her warning went unheeded. "They tutor some elementary-school kids during the week at Dad's church," she added.

"No kidding? Good guys, then. No wonder Jake's impressed with them."

"I'm impressed, too," Beth said, joining her siblings. "They've been great with the little kids. This has been a delightful evening for me. It's so nice not having to chase after the girls every second."

"The boys are patient with the little kids, but then, they all have younger ones in their families."

Will strolled away and Emily faced her sister, who smiled. "This really has been a super evening and I'm glad to see things are better for you and Jake."

"What makes you think that?" Emily asked in surprise.

"Don't tell me they're not! You look far happier. You have

a sparkle in your eyes and Jake can't take his eyes off you. He watches you constantly."

"That doesn't necessarily mean what you think it does. I think we're playing games with each other."

"Look again, Emily. That man is in love with you. He looks like he's done everything possible to make this the best evening ever. That's not game playing. No man will go to lengths like that unless he's really captivated. He's even cozying up to Mom and Dad and listening to Dad's old tales. As a matter of fact, Jake's spent time with everyone in the family and been his charming best. Emily, forgive him for what he did. He deceived you when you married, but he's obviously sorry now. It's equally obvious he cares. Bury the hatchet and you'll live happily ever after."

Emily's inside twisted. "How I wish it were that simple!"

"I don't think you're really looking at your husband. Emily, he adores you. How could you think about walking out on a man who dotes on you, much less one that half the eligible women in Texas would kill for. Emily, you have it all. Open your eyes."

Emily smiled, knowing she'd never convince her sister that things weren't so black and white. There was no point in trying. She was certain Jake was not a man in love. He was after an inheritance, and when he wanted something, he was single-minded and scheming. But he was changing, she realized, or he never would have invited the boys he coached to the party tonight. Just inviting her family would have pleased her.

She glanced across the terrace at Jake. Every time she'd glanced his way tonight, he'd met her gaze. She still felt he was courting her with the cool calculation of a financial acquisition and with just as much heart. Perhaps less.

Beth glanced around. "I think your husband wants to talk to you. See you later," she said, and was gone before Emily could protest. She looked around to see Jake strolling toward her.

"Having a good time?" Jake asked.

"Yes. So is everyone else. Orlando said you're a cool dude."

"Good. I'm glad this party didn't come after the first time I met those kids. That isn't what he would have said about me."

"You might've been surprised. He told me that week that you were 'all right.' Pretty high praise from a teenager."

"You didn't tell me."

She shrugged. "I didn't think you'd care. You must've been able to hold your own with the four of them. I don't think anything short of that would have gained his approval."

"You knew that when you set me up with them," he said.

"Sure. But I also knew you'd win them over, which you did."

"Emily, you could've easily gotten me killed or left out there on that field unconscious."

She laughed. "That's a difficult image to conjure up. I was supremely confident that you'd succeed. One way or another. Oh, and thanks for serving them soda and not beer."

"We discussed that ahead of time," he replied, reaching to rest his hand on her shoulder and rub lightly, a faint contact that shouldn't stir desire, but did. She inhaled and saw that he was watching her intently. "I thought it was wise for them to have soda and they agreed. Want to go help me select another bottle of wine from the wine cellar?" he asked.

"I think I'll stay with our guests," she replied, knowing wine wasn't on Jake's mind. He wanted to get her alone so he could kiss her.

He shifted his hand on her shoulder, still kneading lightly.

"Tonight has been really special, Em. And it's not over yet," he said softly.

Her mouth became dry as she recalled the passionate moments they'd shared before coming downstairs. With an effort she looked away. "Everyone seems to be having a great time." Her voice was breathless and his hand still kneaded her shoulder.

"I told the boys there were swimsuits in the cabana they could have if they wanted to swim. That's where they are now—changing."

She glanced at the pool. Will and Orlando had changed to their swimsuits. "That's great. I doubt any of them get to swim often."

"You and I could swim, too. But I'd rather talk to your dad now and swim when I'm alone with you. Of course, if you want to swim, I'd be happy to watch, but not in that black suit you wore on the island."

"I hardly think so! I wouldn't wear that in front of anyone except you," she said. He chuckled as he gave her shoulder a final squeeze and walked away to talk to her dad.

She joined her mother and watched all the swimmers. The kids took everyone's attention and she was pleased to see all four boys interacting and playing with her nieces and nephew.

Finally everyone climbed out and dressed, and food was served on the veranda. She sat at a table with her dad and her sister and her sister's family.

By the time the meal was over, the kids were hanging on the four boys, who gave them all the attention they wanted. They all left for the game room and the men followed, she guessed to go to the billiards room. The boys seemed relaxed. They had moved enough as kids that they made friends easily. And she knew all her family liked people and enjoyed getting to know them, so it was no surprise that everyone was getting along.

The evening passed quickly and soon the sun had set. Finally the boys thanked Jake and her, said their farewells and left. Next, her siblings gathered up their kids and said good night.

Her parents were the last to leave. When her father hugged her, he smiled and said, "You married a nice guy, Em. I'm glad."

Biting back the hurt his words caused, she returned his hug. Her family had no idea how intense Jake's love of money and power was and to what lengths he would go to get what he wanted.

As her parents' car disappeared down the drive, she turned with Jake to go back into the mansion. Her pulse was already fluttery—she could recall their wild and hasty lovemaking earlier, a frantic loving that had only whetted her desire for him. And she remembered what he had told her just before the party started.

She moved away from him. "That was a great evening. The boys gave all their attention to my nieces and nephew, so they might not have gotten to play pool."

"I'll have them over sometime again when the little kids aren't here and they can do what they want."

"You will?" she asked, surprised. Was he doing all this as part of his campaign of seduction? It was working quite well for him, she had to admit. "I suppose you've taken care of the caterer and everyone else and I don't have to do a thing."

"That's right," he replied.

"It was a wonderful night. Thank you, Jake."

"Sure. I had a great time, too," he said.

She turned and hurried away. She didn't hear him move, so he had to be standing there, watching her. Her back tingled. She was surprised that he had let her go without trying to kiss her. She tried to ignore the streak of disappointment she felt. She passed the splashing three-tier fountain in the entryway and hurried down a hall to go back upstairs to her bedroom.

That was too easy, too unlike Jake. She'd thought she'd have to fight him off once the party ended. She shrugged away her questions, realizing he'd made life easier for her.

Easier and more miserable at the same time. She wanted him more than ever. She knew part of her desire was her happiness at Jake's inviting the boys to the house and getting along so well with them. He intended to invite them back. She wondered if he meant what he said. Time would tell.

She closed the door of her bedroom and switched on a small table lamp. She glanced at the door and memories of earlier returned, of Jake leaning against it, aroused and ready to love.

Taking a deep breath, she tried to focus again on the party while she got her blue silk pajamas and headed for her bathroom. She decided she might sleep better if she had a quick shower. Tomorrow was Sunday. She could leave for church, avoid seeing Jake and put back the distance that they'd had between them.

Yet erotic images of earlier kept taunting her. She wondered how long it would be before she slept. She could go down to swim laps in the pool. But if she did, Jake would probably see her and come outside. And then she'd be hopelessly lost again.

She showered and stepped out to dry and pull on the pajamas, feeling the soft material on her skin. She brushed her hair and turned to leave the room, but halted in the doorway.

Jake was in her bed. Bare-chested. He wore only his jeans. He swung his long legs off the bed and stood.

"What are you doing in here?" she asked.

"I knocked and when you didn't answer, I came in to wait until you finished your shower," he said, walking to her. Her heart thudded more intensely with each step closer he came. "You look luscious," he drawled in the husky tone he always got when he was aroused.

"Jake, we already said good night," she reminded him. He took the towel from her hands and flung it aside, then wrapped his arms around her and pulled her to him.

She pushed against his chest. His hands slid down to her waist. "We're not going to do this," she said. "In spite of what we did earlier, nothing in our relationship has changed." It was a major effort to get the words out.

"Whatever you want. But I don't think a kiss will cause disaster."

"You won't stop with a kiss," she whispered, knowing she wouldn't, either.

"I can and I will if that's what you want," he said. "If we can't kiss, then let's just talk."

"You don't really want to talk," she said.

"Em, I've been thinking about letting Orlando work with my gardener, Holz," Jake said, in another surprise. She blinked and stared at him, amazed by this new twist.

"I think Orlando could help with yard work and he could work part-time, earn a little more money."

"Jake! That's absolutely wonderful!" she exclaimed, deciding she wasn't going to worry about Jake's motives. At the moment the intent of Jake's offer wasn't as significant as the end result. "That's fantastic! Oh, Jake…" She was torn between throwing her arms around his neck in gratitude and remembering all her reservations and promises to herself.

He didn't give her the choice. He pulled her to him and she wound her arms around his neck. "Damn you for being irresistible! And doing things you know I'll be thrilled about," she said. "That's the most wonderful present you've ever given me!"

"Em, it's nothing," he said, shaking his head. "He's a smart strong kid, and he'll be a good worker. I'm being nice to him, is all. Why didn't you tell me he gets straight A's? And Anthony almost does."

"I didn't think that would matter to you. You were only going to coach them in football."

"All four are smart kids. Tanek and Enzo are going to do well. The only problem they have right now is adjusting to a new culture, and Enzo needs to work on his English. I expect both of them to get top grades."

"The school is trying to help get Orlando and Anthony college scholarships. But the school needs help. I donated some of your money to the athletic department and to the band—their equipment is terrible."

"I'll ask Orlando and Anthony about their scholarships. If Orlando comes to work here, I figured I might as well find something for Anthony to do, too. He's going to work for Holz doing landscaping and gardening."

"You're hiring both Anthony and Orlando?" she asked, overjoyed by the news.

"Yes. The other two are juniors and busy with activities and their families, so they don't need jobs."

She remembered that first Saturday when Jake had returned filled with anger and announced they would have killed him if they could. "I knew you'd win their friendship! Jake, I'm so happy that you're hiring Orlando and Anthony."

"They're both high-school football players and I have to find out what the rules are during the school year about them having jobs, but we'll work it out. The craziest things please you. No diamonds I've given you have ever put the sparkle in your eyes that offering to hire Orlando as a gardener has done."

Tears threatened to fall down Emily's cheeks. She was so happy and relieved to see that Jake had bonded with the boys. She had never been able to tell Jake that she thought he'd lost sight of what he could really do to help others the way he'd been helped. And now the boys had broken through Jake's self-absorption, and she was overjoyed.

"Em?" Jake held her shoulders and bent his knees slightly to look into her eyes. "Do I see tears?" he asked in amazement.

She tried to blink them back. "No, I'm just happy. You've made me so happy. This party, my family here, your making friends with the boys...."

"Makes me wonder how you saw me when we got married. You sound as if I've gone from a three-headed monster to Mr. Nice Guy."

"You can be Mr. Nice Guy when you want to be," she said, wiping her eyes and smiling at him. Her smile faded when she looked into his smoldering gaze.

"Those pajamas cover too much," he said, and leaned down to kiss her. He wrapped his arms around her, pulling her close while he kissed her.

She stood still, her hands against his chest. She knew she should push him away—he'd release her at the first indication she wanted him to stop—but she could only kiss him in return. In seconds, her arms wound around his neck.

He reached beneath her pajama top to cup her breast and caress her nipple, rubbing her with his thumb, and she knew she couldn't walk away from his touch.

\* \* \*

They made love through the night. It was dawn when she finally lay quietly in his arms. "Jake, this doesn't change things between us," she said, but the words sounded empty.

"We'll just take each day as it comes. I want you to move back into our bedroom, Em," he said, turning on his side and propping his head on his hand while he toyed with locks of her hair. "I want you with me."

"No. You know you can seduce me and I melt, but I'm not ready to go back to the way things were. And I don't want to get pregnant. I still expect this marriage to end before the year is out."

"I hope that doesn't happen," he said solemnly, but she wondered what he truly felt.

"You could have gotten pregnant tonight. That didn't seem to worry you."

"What are the odds on that? I'm not changing my mind."

He nuzzled her neck. "All right. This has been a fantastic night," he whispered, tracing the curve of her ear with his tongue, making her skin tingle once again. She wrapped her arm around his neck and smiled at him, combing her fingers through his thick hair.

"Yes, it has been. You're tossing it away with both hands, Jake. The time will soon come when I'll go. I'm not staying in this marriage."

"Before you do, think it through and reconsider leaving."

She shook her head. "No. I can't continue the way things are."

He gazed into her blue eyes and her pulse drummed. His expression was somber. "I want you, Em," he whispered, and looked at her mouth. Her heart thudded and her nipples tightened, heat pooling low in her belly. She should stop him, but he was too seductive. His head came down, his mouth covered hers and she held him tightly and kissed him in return. Tonight was lost. She would deal with getting Jake out of her life later.

In spite of feeling he'd made real progress in smoothing things over with Emily, Jake didn't see her the following week. Winning the boys' friendship had been the one bright spot—it had caused her to let down her barriers. He had to come up with more reasons to be with her and more ways he could destroy those barriers completely. Since that night, she'd been less angry with him and more receptive. But now he barely saw her and suspected she was staying away until late at night.

He'd had to go to France for business and went to see Hub while he was in Europe. The old man had slipped badly and could barely talk to him. Jake stayed only a few minutes and then talked to the nurse. Hub's condition was worsening daily.

Jake knew he ought to give up even thinking about the inheritance. Emily wasn't pregnant and didn't want to be. If things didn't change between them, she'd get out of the marriage in a little over five months. He might as well resign himself to the situation. He'd never had a relationship with any other woman that had lasted as long as his already had with Emily. The way he felt right now, he wasn't going to be ready for her to walk out of his life. Perhaps he would when the time came, but he doubted it. Emily intrigued him, continually surprised him. He liked to be with her. And the sex was fabulous. If he stopped to think about it, he'd never been as fascinated with any other woman. When he'd proposed, he'd thought he was getting a quiet cooperative wife who would stay in the background of his life, give him an heir and do what he wanted. His miscalculation had been monumental, but exciting. Just thinking about her made him want to see her. She wouldn't take his calls, and he suspected he wasn't going to see her when he returned home for the weekend.

While courting Emily, he'd let business slide and he was trying to catch up. After the week in Europe, he flew to Tokyo. From there he had dealings in Malaysia, and then flew home from there.

He would have to return to Paris, but after that he was determined to stay home and make sure he and Emily spent time together. He intended to check into going to her dad's church for the Wednesday-night tutoring. *I must be really getting desperate to be with her,* he thought.

He figured he'd have to have her family over again. He wondered if they had any birthdays coming up. Emily wouldn't tell him, but her sister would. He decided when he got home from work, he'd call Beth and ask.

Thoughts of Emily were distracting him at work. His concentration was shot. He'd never had that happen before. If they could just make love, he thought, all the sizzling fantasies would vanish—he could sleep nights, instead of tossing and turning, dreaming about her.

He entered his house, pulling off his jacket and tie. It was Monday and he hadn't seen Emily even for an hour for over three weeks. He didn't want to spend the night in his big empty mansion alone.

He passed the library and heard a sound. He glanced into the darkened room. He was startled to see Emily in a wing chair, sitting and staring out the window. She wiped her eyes with a tissue and he wondered if something had happened to someone in her family.

"Emily?" he said, dropping his jacket and tie on a chair as his concern grew. He switched on a light and she turned her head.

Her eyes and nose were red and tears streamed down her cheeks. Her lap was filled with balled-up tissues, and a box of tissues sat beside her chair.

"Emily, what in heaven's name?" he asked, cold with fear. "Has something happened? Is anyone hurt? What's wrong?" He rushed to kneel beside her and take her hand.

She yanked her hand away. Rage blazed in her eyes. "Get away from me!" she snapped.

Startled, he stood and stepped back. With his hands on his hips, he stared at her. "What is it? What the hell is wrong?"

She looked up at him and he saw that if she'd had anything in her hands, she would have thrown it at him. He had seldom seen such fury in anyone's eyes.

"You won!" she said in a low tight voice, laced with rage. "You always win. The entire world does what you want. Go get your damned inheritance! I'm pregnant. You can claim your billions. And when Hubert Braden dies, I'm leaving you," she added bitterly. "You'll have what you wanted."

# Ten

"I'm going to be a father!" Jake exclaimed, stunned. Now that it had actually happened, he was amazed. "A father," he repeated, unable to fully grasp this monumental change in his life.

His heart thudded violently as he stared at her. Emily was carrying his baby! He wanted to hug and kiss her. But he didn't dare touch her. And he would get Hub's inheritance! She was pregnant! Jubilation surged, but he also knew he didn't dare exhibit any enthusiasm around her.

"Have you seen a doctor?"

"Yes."

"Emily—"

"Don't!" she exclaimed, waving her hand at him. "Don't talk to me. Don't say another word. Get out of my sight. Go claim your inheritance. Just stay away from me. I don't want to see you or talk to you." She turned to look out the window, ending the conversation.

He stared at her a moment and decided he would do what she wanted. She had months to calm down. He would try to soothe things over later. Now he snatched up his jacket and tie and raced for the study to call Hub. He couldn't talk to the old man, but he could tell his nurse to let him know. He could call Hub's accountant and the attorney who had written the will.

He was going to be a dad! In spite of trying for this for well over a year, he was amazed now that it had happened. He would get the inheritance! At least a billion dollars!

As he called Hub, he thought about calling his mother. She'd tell him that she was happy for him, but he wasn't certain she'd be thrilled to learn she'd be a grandmother. She was not into kids and babies. His money had transformed her life completely—she drove a Jaguar, spent half the year on the French Riviera or in Paris and part of the time in New York. She liked to party and gamble, and had put her past life as far behind her as she could. He also thought about calling his sister, Nina. But she was an unmarried attorney, not overly interested in children, so he didn't think he'd get much enthusiasm there, either.

The people who would be happy were Emily's family, but he couldn't call them. He had to leave that to her. He thought about Emily alone in the library, crying and angry. He regretted her reaction, but he had to do what she wanted and leave her alone.

He put away his cell phone. He'd fly to Europe and tell Hub himself. Then he could let the accountant and attorney know. He wanted to see the old man's face and give him the pleasure of knowing there was a baby on the way.

Jake called his pilot and made arrangements for a flight early in the morning.

Next, he called a florist and ordered an enormous bouquet of tulips, carnations and daisies for Emily. She probably wouldn't like it, but he wanted her to have it. He'd make a donation to her father's church in her honor, which hopefully might really please her and celebrate the occasion. He grinned and looked into space, thinking about their baby.

He would be a father. The idea, now that it had become a fact, amazed him more than ever. He didn't know anything about babies or children, but Emily did. He wondered if she was still sitting in the library, crying. He hoped she would get over her anger soon.

In the meantime, he decided it would be best if he stayed out of her way.

The library grew darker as the sun set. Emily wasn't aware of her surroundings. After more than a year of trying to get pregnant, it happened when she didn't want it to happen anymore. She was going to have Jake's baby. All she could think about, though, was that Jake would get the inheritance.

He didn't care about her or his baby. Just the money. And once again, Jake got what he wanted in life. She wiped her eyes. She was certain he had gone racing off to call Hubert Braden. Already, some attorney in Switzerland or New York or wherever Hubert Braden did business would be planning for the bulk of the estate to go to Jake.

She would stay, have the baby, and the minute Hubert Braden died, she would leave Jake. She wasn't going to leave him now and deprive him of the inheritance he craved so badly. If his life was wrapped up in acquiring money, then she would no longer stand in his way.

More hot tears streamed down her cheeks. She'd fallen in

love with Jake. He didn't know it and never would, but she had. He was desirable, irresistible. But his willingness to help the boys and his interest in them had won her heart. In spite of that, she didn't want to stay and spend her life with a man who put money above all else.

Money was more important to Jake than family. Emily knew she would have to tell *her* family the news, but she was waiting until she'd become accustomed to the idea of a baby. And she wouldn't let her family know she intended to leave Jake. They'd find out when the time came. The baby was due next June. She would stay that first year, but then she would get away from Jake and his greed.

In the meantime, as soon as she could pull herself together, she would let her family know. They would support her, shower their love and joy on her. She wiped her eyes and thought about calling Beth and going to see her later this week. Things would be okay.

She was going to have Jake's baby. She stood and went up to her room by the back stairs, hoping to avoid Jake. She succeeded.

She sank into a chair in her room and stared into space, lost in thought about the coming months.

"Emily? Emily?"

She stared at the door without answering.

"Can I bring you dinner? You should eat," he called.

"No," she replied, and hoped he'd go away.

"Let me know if you need anything," he said.

She didn't bother to answer. Later, she stretched out on the bed and fell into a troubled sleep.

The next morning, she stirred as someone placed a blanket over her. It was dusky in the room, still before dawn.

She opened her eyes to see Jake straightening the blanket over her.

"What are you doing?" she asked.

"Sorry if I woke you. I brought you a tray with some juice, a glass of milk and a small pot of tea. There's toast if you can eat it. I thought you'd like a blanket."

"I'm fine, Jake," she replied stiffly. He wore a navy suit with a red tie, so he must have stopped in before heading to work.

"I'm going to Europe, Emily. I'll be in Paris tonight." She looked at him, barely listening, knowing whatever he was doing overseas, he would go see Hubert Braden and tell him about the baby. She turned away.

He brushed her cheek with a kiss. "Take care of yourself. I'll be back in three days."

"Goodbye, Jake."

He frowned and left, closing the door behind him. She looked at the tray, realizing she hadn't eaten since yesterday morning. She sat up and drank the juice.

An hour later she walked into the nursery and gazed at the storybook murals on the walls, the white furniture and bookshelves, the circular Mother Goose throw rugs. Then, closing the door behind her, she walked back to the room adjoining the bedroom she now occupied. She'd wait until she knew whether she was having a boy or girl and have the nursery done over.

She had managed to avoid Jake these past few weeks, and she suspected that now, he would no longer try to find reasons to be with her. She wondered if he would stop coaching the boys. At least Orlando and Anthony worked for them—that wouldn't change. And the baby would always be well taken care of. She wondered if Jake had any interest in his baby. No, he was only interested in himself. She was certain he was on his way now to claim the inheritance.

Jake gazed out the window of the jet. With his mind jumping from the inheritance to becoming a father to Emily, he couldn't concentrate on work. As he looked at mounds of clouds far below, he thought about his future.

When he returned from this trip and the inheritance was his, he would lose Emily. That bothered him. She wouldn't back down on her threat. Once the inheritance became his, she would leave him. And he couldn't fight her for his child. He would never do that to her.

He shifted uncomfortably. He wasn't ready for Emily to leave him. She had become important to him. He wanted her to stay.

Idly rubbing his knee, he thought about her smiling at him, throwing her arms around him when he'd told her he'd given Orlando a job.

Emily was going to have his baby and then exit his life.

He knew he could marry again, but he would never find anyone like Emily. His family had been dysfunctional, his father uncaring and his mother too busy trying to keep food on the table to shower love on him and his sister. Jake had helped raise his sister, but they weren't anything like the loving siblings Emily had.

With Emily he could have a family like hers. But was Emily worth giving up a billion-dollar inheritance?

He rubbed his knee again. He was worth more than a billion already. As Emily had pointed out, he didn't actually need the money. Why did he want it if he lost Emily?

Startled, Jake frowned and looked out the window again.

He was in love with his wife. He didn't know when it had happened, but he loved her.

He thought about the fortune he would inherit now. He didn't want to give it up, yet he damn well wasn't ready to give up Emily. He raked his fingers through his hair and swore under his breath.

The pilot announced their approach to Charles de Gaulle International Airport. Jake folded his briefcase, put away his calculator and gazed out the window, still lost in thought and not seeing anything below.

Jake thought about the future, weighing his options and possibilities. When the jet landed, he rode in a waiting limousine to the hotel suite he'd reserved and made some calls, canceling appointments he had set up for tomorrow. He'd intended to go straight to Switzerland from Paris to see Hub, but now he wanted to think things through and make sure he wasn't doing something he would regret the rest of his life.

By Wednesday, Emily's spirits had improved. Excitement filled her when she thought about telling her family about the baby. At this point, she'd still have to include Jake when she told them, but her brother and dad would get Jake off to themselves and she'd have her mother and sister fussing over the pregnancy. And they would all be thrilled. Each new Carlisle baby was welcomed with open arms by the entire family. She smiled, thinking about it, knowing she didn't care whether she had a boy or girl. She just wanted a healthy baby.

She invited her family for dinner a week from Friday, feeling by then she'd have gotten a grip on her emotions. They could get another dinner catered, and she could make her announcement.

She spent the day making plans and calls, getting her family members to put the date on their calendars and booking one of Jake's caterers.

On Thursday morning, she went shopping for something special for the baby. Just one or two things to make it all real to her. It was midafternoon when she arrived home, trying to avoid thinking about Jake. He should have his inheritance lined up by now.

She stretched out on her bed for a nap. She'd given the household staff the week off since Jake was gone, so she had the house to herself.

When the phone rang, she answered, thinking it might be her sister calling to make plans to get together. Instead, it was Hubert Braden's nurse, and she sat up and listened.

The old man had lapsed into a coma and he wasn't expected to rally. Jake had been there and gone and they couldn't get in touch with him. So they'd called his home, though they would keep trying to get him on his cell.

Emily promised to make sure Jake knew as soon as she could get hold of him. The nurse was so thankful Jake had been to see Mr. Braden while the old man was still conscious.

The connection ended and Emily stared into space. With Jake's luck, he'd made it in time to tell Hubert Braden himself. She shook her head. If she hadn't gotten pregnant now, Jake wouldn't get the inheritance. Hubert Braden wasn't going to last and the money would have been distributed primarily to charities.

Because of her succumbing to Jake's charm, Jake would

have his fortune almost doubled. She looked around the elegant bedroom with its expensive furnishings and shook her head. She hoped Jake enjoyed his money. But he'd have to enjoy it alone. Although, with a baby between them, she'd be involved with Jake on some level for the next twenty years or so.

With a sigh, she got up to put away her purchases—a baby blanket, a stuffed bear and a bath toy, little things she couldn't resist because they made the coming event seem more real.

On Friday she hoped to leave the house early in the afternoon so she could avoid seeing Jake when he arrived.

She showered and dressed in tan slacks and a beige blouse, picking up her bag to go, when she heard Jake's footsteps in the hall.

He knocked and opened the door. "Emily?"

He'd already shed his tie and unbuttoned the top buttons of his shirt. Tangled locks of black hair fell over his forehead. As handsome as ever, the sight of him made her pulse race. He stepped into the room and smiled at her. "You look beautiful, Em," he said warmly.

"Your timing was perfect, Jake," she said. "Hubert Braden's nurse called and said they were trying to get in touch with you. She said you'd been there and talked to him. You told him about the baby just in time. Mr. Braden has lapsed into a coma, and they don't expect him to regain consciousness. They don't think he'll last more than a day or two."

Jake closed his eyes and looked pained for a moment. She was surprised. Was Hubert Braden the one person in the world Jake truly cared about?

"I'm sorry," she said. "But at least you got your inheritance just in the nick of time."

"Em, I want to talk to you about that." Jake crossed the room to put his hands on her shoulders.

She stiffened and gazed at him solemnly, wondering what he was after now. His gray eyes were intense.

"I didn't tell him we're expecting a baby," Jake said quietly.

She stared at Jake, unable to comprehend what he was telling her. "Why? Why would you do that?" she asked.

"I love you," he declared, and her heart thudded. "On the flight to Paris, I had time to think about it. If I got that inheritance, I'd lose you. But I realized I'm in love with you. I don't want you to go."

Stunned, she stared at him. "You really aren't getting the inheritance?" she whispered.

"No, I'm not. I gave up a fortune for you. I thought about what you'd said. I don't really need it. But I do need you. Em, I love you and I want you and our baby."

She blinked as he leaned down to look more intently at her. "Emily, I love you."

"Oh, Jake!" She threw her arms around him, crying and laughing and kissing him wildly. Her heart raced and she couldn't quite believe she'd heard him right. She leaned back to hold his face. "You're telling me the truth? You're really not going to let Hubert Braden's lawyer know about the baby?"

"I won't if you won't. We won't tell anyone while they settle the will. Then the money will be given to Hub's favorite charities and we can announce that we're having a baby to the world."

He wound his hand in her hair and tilted her head back. "I need you more than any fortune. I'd toss it all for you," he said. He leaned down to kiss her and she clung to him, overjoyed, unable to believe what was happening. She leaned back to hold his face again so he would look at her. "Jake, I love you!" she said, then stood on tiptoe to continue kissing him.

He picked her up, holding her close in his arms and carrying her to bed, while he showered kisses on her and proved his love.

# Epilogue

*One month later*

Jake's mountain home in Colorado was everything Emily had imagined. A fire roared in the enormous stone fireplace and three handsome dark-haired men stood in front of it, laughing and talking.

Warmth filled her when she looked at Jake, and she knew the feeling wasn't from the blaze on the hearth, but from the love she had for her husband. She turned her attention back to the women sitting with her. Blond Ashley Warner had been her wedding planner and truly a friend through that hectic period. Nick Colton's wife, Abby, sat at her other side. Red-haired and beautiful, Abby was friendly and delightful. Emily was happy to renew her friendships with Abby and Ashley. Jake had planned a week at his mountain retreat and he'd invited his friends to come and stay over on Saturday so they wouldn't have to navigate mountain roads late at night to get back to their *own* homes.

And his mountain home with its twelve bedrooms was almost as palatial as his Dallas mansion, so there was plenty of room for three families.

"When we get back home, you'll both have to come visit and meet Ben," Ashley said. "He's a little over a year now and beginning to toddle. Both of you can come see what fun you're in for."

Emily smiled at Abby, who had announced that she and Nick were expecting a baby next July. "I brought baby-name books to look at while we were traveling," Emily said, and Abby laughed. "I have a suitcase filled with them. We'll wait to design a nursery when we know what we're having."

"We have a nursery, thanks to Jake's overeagerness," Emily said, smiling.

The friends had come early in the day so the men could spend time together and catch up on their news. As Ashley and Abby talked, Emily looked at Jake's large family room with soaring twenty-foot ceilings, wood-paneled walls and polished hardwood floors. The house had wings in both directions and was nestled in the mountains near his friends' luxurious mountain getaways.

She looked at Jake again in his thick cable-knit sweater, khakis and boots. He looked relaxed and handsome, and she was ready to be alone with him again.

He met her gaze, holding it for a long moment before he turned his attention back to his friends.

As if she'd whispered in his ear, a short time later Jake offered nightcaps, which his friends both declined, saying they would turn in for the night.

She stood with Jake's arm around her while the Coltons and the Warners disappeared upstairs to the east wing. The master bedroom was in the opposite wing.

When Jake turned her to face him, she wrapped her arms around his neck. "Your friends are wonderful. It's great to see Ashley and Abby again and get to know them better."

"Good. I've wanted to bring you here and get together with them."

A log cracked in the fireplace, sending up dancing orange sparks. She looked back into Jake's eyes and her heart thudded with joy. "I love you so much, Jake," she whispered.

"It scares me to think how close I came to losing you because of my own blindness. Emily, I want to do everything possible to make you happy."

She kissed his cheek, feeling the faint stubble. "I can think of something you can do," she whispered.

Jake's eyes darkened and he looked at her mouth. "Let's go upstairs," he said. You go ahead and I'll wind things up here."

"I'll go slip into something I know you'll like."

"Just slip out of what you're wearing and I'll be happy," he said. "I built a fire earlier so the room will be toasty."

"Don't take long, Jake," she said in a sultry voice, her pulse skipping in anticipation.

He smiled and turned away to lock up. She hurried upstairs to put on the black negligee Jake had bought her in Paris. A fire still burned in the large stone fireplace at one end of the bedroom. The king-size bed was turned down and she wondered when Jake had come up and gotten things ready.

Eagerly, she waited, climbing on the bed and pulling the sheet to her chin. Finally he stepped through the door and crossed the room to the bed to sit down and yank off his boots. He turned to her. "Come here," he said in a raspy voice, pulling her into his embrace and shoving away the sheet.

"Ahh," he said in satisfaction, then stood, pulling her up so he could look at her in the sheer negligee. "You're stunning, Em."

She laughed and stepped into his arms, winding hers around his neck. "I have the sexiest, most handsome husband in the world," she said, rubbing against him and standing on tiptoe to kiss him.

Jake wrapped her in his embrace and leaned over her to kiss her passionately, and Emily's heart pounded with joy. She loved her tall sexy husband and she knew he loved her. She expected a bright future filled with a family they could nurture and love.

\* \* \* \* \*

*The Colton family is back!*
*Enjoy a sneak preview of*
*COLTON'S SECRET SERVICE*
*by Marie Ferrarella, part of*
**THE COLTONS: FAMILY FIRST** *miniseries.*
*Available from Silhouette Romantic Suspense*
*in September 2008.*

He cautioned himself to be leery. He was human and he'd been conned before. But never by anyone nearly so attractive. Never by anyone he'd felt so attracted to.

In her defense, Nick supposed that Georgie could actually be telling him the truth. That she was a victim in all this. He had his people back in California checking her out, to make sure she was who she said she was and had, as she claimed, not even been near a computer but on the road these last few months that the threats had been made.

In the meantime, he was doing his own checking out. Up close and exceedingly personal. So personal he could feel his blood stirring.

It had been a long time since he'd thought of himself as anything other than a law enforcement agent of one type or other. But Georgeann Grady made him remember that beneath the oaths he had taken and his devotion to duty, there beat the heart of a man.

A man who'd been far too long without the touch of a woman.

He watched as the light from the fireplace caressed the outline of Georgie's small, trim, jean-clad body as she moved about the rustic living room that could have easily come off the set of a Hollywood Western. Except that it was genuine.

As genuine as she claimed to be?

Something inside of him hoped so.

He wasn't supposed to be taking sides. His only interest in being here was to guarantee Senator Joe Colton's safety as the latter continued to make his bid for the presidency. Everything else was supposed to be secondary, but, Nick had to silently admit, that was just a wee bit hard to remember right now.

Earlier, before she'd put her precocious handful of a daughter to bed, Georgie had fed his appetite by whipping up some kind of a delicious concoction out of the vegetables she'd pulled from her garden. Vegetables that, by all rights, should have been withered and dried. She'd mentioned that a friend came by on occasion to weed and tend it. Still, it surprised him that somehow she'd managed to make something mouth-watering out of it.

Almost as mouthwatering as she looked to him right at this moment.

Again, he was reminded of the appetite that hadn't been fed, hadn't been satisfied.

And wasn't going to be, Nick sternly told himself. At least not now. Maybe later, when things took on a more definite shape and all the questions in his head were answered to his satisfaction, there would be time to explore this feeling. This woman. But not now.

Damn it.

"Sorry about the lack of light," Georgie said, breaking into his train of thought as she turned around to face him. If she noticed the way he was looking at her, she gave no indication. "But I don't see a point in paying for electricity if I'm not going to be here. Besides, Emmie really enjoys camping out. She likes roughing it."

"And you?" Nick asked, moving closer to her, so close that a whisper would have trouble fitting in. "What do you like?"

The very breath stopped in Georgie's throat as she looked up at him.

"I think you've got a fair shot of guessing that one," she told him softly.

\* \* \* \* \*

*Be sure to look for COLTON'S SECRET SERVICE*
*and the other following titles from*
**THE COLTONS: FAMILY FIRST** *miniseries:*
*RANCHER'S REDEMPTION by Beth Cornelison*
*THE SHERIFF'S AMNESIAC BRIDE by Linda Conrad*
*SOLDIER'S SECRET CHILD by Caridad Piñeiro*
*BABY'S WATCH by Justine Davis*
*A HERO OF HER OWN by Carla Cassidy*

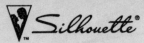

## Romantic

# SUSPENSE

**Sparked by Danger,
Fueled by Passion.**

### The Coltons Are Back!

# Marie Ferrarella

## *Colton's Secret Service*

### The Coltons: Family First

On a mission to protect a senator, Secret Service agent Nick Sheffield tracks down a threatening message only to discover Georgie Gradie Colton, a rodeo-riding single mom, who insists on her innocence. Nick is instantly taken with the feisty redhead, but vows not to let his feelings interfere with his mission. Now he must figure out if this woman is conning him or if he can trust her and the passion they share....

**Available September wherever books are sold.**

**Look for upcoming Colton titles
from Silhouette Romantic Suspense:**

RANCHER'S REDEMPTION by Beth Cornelison, Available October
THE SHERIFF'S AMNESIAC BRIDE by Linda Conrad, Available November
SOLDIER'S SECRET CHILD by Caridad Piñeiro, Available December
BABY'S WATCH by Justine Davis, Available January 2009
A HERO OF HER OWN by Carla Cassidy, Available February 2009

**Visit Silhouette Books at www.eHarlequin.com**    SRS27598

# HQN™

## We *are* romance™

**He's getting under her skin…in more ways than one.**

**From *New York Times* bestselling author**

# Susan Andersen

Jane thought nothing could make her lose her cool. But she blows a gasket the night she meets the contractor restoring the Wolcott mansion. Devlin Kavanagh's rugged sex appeal may buckle her knees, but she won't tolerate theatrics from someone hired to work on the house she has just inherited.

Dev could renovate the mansion in his sleep. But ever since Jane spotted him jet-lagged, she's been on his case. Yet there's something about her. Jane hides behind conservative clothes and a frosty manner, but her seductive blue eyes and leopard-print heels hint at a woman just dying to cut loose!

## Cutting Loose

**Catch this sexy new title in stores this August!**

**www.HQNBooks.com**

PHSA304

# REQUEST YOUR FREE BOOKS!

## 2 FREE NOVELS PLUS 2 FREE GIFTS!

### Passionate, Powerful, Provocative!

**YES!** Please send me 2 FREE Silhouette Desire® novels and my 2 FREE gifts (gifts are worth about $10). After receiving them, if I don't wish to receive any more books, I can return the shipping statement marked "cancel". If I don't cancel, I will receive 6 brand-new novels every month and be billed just $4.05 per book in the U.S. or $4.74 per book in Canada, plus 25¢ shipping and handling per book and applicable taxes, if any*. That's a savings of almost 15% off the cover price! I understand that accepting the 2 free books and gifts places me under no obligation to buy anything. I can always return a shipment and cancel at any time. Even if I never buy another book, the two free books and gifts are mine to keep forever.        225 SDN ERVX  326 SDN ERVM

Name _____ (PLEASE PRINT) _____

Address _____ Apt. # _____

City _____ State/Prov. _____ Zip/Postal Code _____

Signature (if under 18, a parent or guardian must sign)

### Mail to the Silhouette Reader Service:
**IN U.S.A.:** P.O. Box 1867, Buffalo, NY  14240-1867
**IN CANADA:** P.O. Box 609, Fort Erie, Ontario  L2A 5X3

Not valid to current subscribers of Silhouette Desire books.

### Want to try two free books from another line?
### Call 1-800-873-8635 or visit www.morefreebooks.com.

* Terms and prices subject to change without notice. N.Y. residents add applicable sales tax. Canadian residents will be charged applicable provincial taxes and GST. Offer not valid in Quebec. This offer is limited to one order per household. All orders subject to approval. Credit or debit balances in a customer's account(s) may be offset by any other outstanding balance owed by or to the customer. Please allow 4 to 6 weeks for delivery. Offer available while quantities last.

**Your Privacy:** Silhouette Books is committed to protecting your privacy. Our Privacy Policy is available online at www.eHarlequin.com or upon request from the Reader Service. From time to time we make our lists of customers available to reputable third parties who may have a product or service of interest to you. If you would prefer we not share your name and address, please check here. ☐

SDES08R

*Silhouette* *Desire*

---

## Billionaires and Babies

## MAUREEN CHILD
# BABY BONANZA

Newly single mom Jenna Baker has only
one thing on her mind: child support for
her twin boys. Ship owner and carefree
billionaire Nick Falco discovers he's a
daddy—brought on by a night of passion
a year ago. Nick may be ready to become
a father, but is he ready to become a
groom when he discovers the passion that
still exists between him and Jenna?

**Available September
wherever books are sold.**

**Always Powerful, Passionate and Provocative.**

**Visit Silhouette Books at www.eHarlequin.com**  SD76893

# COMING NEXT MONTH

### #1891 PRINCE OF MIDTOWN—Jennifer Lewis
*Park Avenue Scandals*
This royal had only one way to keep his dedicated—and lovely—
assistant under his roof...seduce her into his bed!

### #1892 THE M.D.'S MISTRESS—Joan Hohl
*Gifts from a Billionaire*
*Finally* she was with the sexy surgeon she'd always loved. But
would their affair last longer than the week?

### #1893 BABY BONANZA—Maureen Child
*Billionaires and Babies*
Secret twin babies? A carefree billionaire discovers he's a
daddy—but is he ready to become a groom?

### #1894 WED BY DECEPTION—Emilie Rose
*The Payback Affairs*
The husband she'd believed dead was back—and very much alive.
And determined to make her his...at any cost.

### #1895 HIS EXPECTANT EX—Catherine Mann
*The Landis Brothers*
The ink was not yet dry on their divorce papers when she
discovered she was pregnant. Could a baby bring them a second
chance?

### #1896 THE DESERT KING—Olivia Gates
*Throne of Judar*
Forced to marry to save his throne, this desert king could not deny
the passion he felt for his bride of *in*convenience.

SDCNM0808